Laura D. Bastian

Winter's KISS

a novel

Lange House Press

Other Books by

Laura D. Bastian

Sink Or Swim

Echoes of Summer

Eye On Orion

Beyond Orion

Heart of Orion

Guardians of the Gate

Cover Design by Novak Illustrations
Edited by Paula Buckendorf
Interior Design by Lange House Press

ISBN-10: 1-944137-04-1

ISBN-13: 978-1-944137-04-5

Chapter One

Carrie hiked up her pencil skirt a few inches to allow her legs to get into the car and cursed herself for sleeping through her alarm. She never should have agreed to the blind date her roommate, Abby, had set her up on last night. The guy was decent enough at first, until he'd had a couple of drinks too many. She should have called him a cab, but hadn't wanted to inconvenience him with a missing car, so she'd driven him home in his own car, then had to ward off his drunken advances as she got him to his apartment. At least he'd passed out on his sofa, and she'd been safe enough as she waited for her cab to show up.

The late night shouldn't have bothered her much, but there had been a few too many recently, and she'd begun to feel it. At least today was Friday, and she could take an easy weekend.

Carrie smiled to herself. If she was truthful, she wouldn't rest this weekend. She was dying to try out the new surfboard she'd saved up for, but the waves weren't expected to be the best. She'd make do. Besides, a trip to the beach would be a perfect way to relax.

But if she didn't hurry, she'd be late for work, and that would never do. As the new account manager at Carlson Ad Agency, she was busier now than she'd ever been as the assistant to Madison Perry-Koholohini. Being one of the youngest at the agency, she wanted to prove to everyone that twenty-four was a reliable adult age.

As she drove in the early morning light on the familiar road leading out of her neighborhood, she was glad the sun was to her back. She'd driven this road so many times over the last few years, so she allowed her mind to wander back to the latest string of failed romances — if she could even call them that. Most guys her age were completely uninterested in anything more than superficial relationships. And she wasn't the kind of girl to agree to one-night stands.

Though she appreciated her looks, long legs, and curves, people often mistook her friendly nature for flirting. She didn't want the superficial though. Her father hadn't been a reliable man, as evidenced by her family. Each of her siblings had a different mother, and now her father was in jail, and she had been made legal guardian for her younger brother, Eric, whose mom had died when he was ten.

Carrie drove on autopilot, following the car in front of her. With the sun angled the way it was, the palm trees glowed, making some look to be lit from within. She studied the different colors of the trees while driving down the road, loving Southern California even more.

As she crossed the intersection behind the car in front of her, tires squealed, a horn blared, and she slammed on her brakes, but not fast enough to avoid crashing into the side of a sleek black sports car.

"No, no, no, no, no." Carrie took stock of herself. The airbag had gone off, sending a cloud of chemicals floating in the car and reflecting the sunlight. She coughed and rubbed her face, feeling the sting of the airbag. Her sunglasses were gone, and she wondered where they'd landed. Wetness slid down her cheek, and she wiped at it with a finger. She stared at the bright red for a few moments, trying to process what had happened.

Someone had run the light and hit her. *Idiot driver.*

With shaking hands, she fumbled in her center console, looking for a tissue or napkin to press against her cheek. Before she found anything useful, a knock on her window brought her attention to the man in a tailored suit standing outside. The look of concern on his face made her smile. Some handsome hero was trying to rescue her, and at the moment, she was completely willing to let him.

She turned to roll the window down, but the car had shut off in the accident, and the window didn't work. When she gripped the handle, pain flashed through her wrist, and she pulled her hand back, cradling it against her chest. The guy knocked on the door again, and she looked up at him.

"What were you thinking?" he asked through the closed window, the look on his face definitely not friendly, like she'd first thought. "Didn't you see the red light?" He looked back at the shiny black car her plain white one had smashed. Carrie shook her head.

"No way," she whispered. "I hit him?" She tried to focus and glanced around the area to get her bearings. The sun was behind her, so she hadn't been blinded by the sun. And the car in front of her had gone through on a green light. How had this happened?

Carrie stared at the angry man who kept talking through the closed window. No, he definitely wasn't a knight in shining armor come to rescue her; he was more like the ogre she needed saving from. She reached across herself to press the lock button. He stopped his tirade and stepped back, making Carrie breathe easier for a bit. She turned to find her purse, but it had fallen to the floor on the passenger side. Her phone had spilled out among a few other things, but she managed to bend over enough to reach it.

She turned it on and called 911 to report the accident and get someone there to help her with this man. She wasn't going to get out until an officer arrived to keep this dragon from eating her alive.

"Nine-one-one, what's your emergency?"

"I've been in an accident." Carrie peered out the windshield to give the dispatcher the address.

"An officer is already en route. Are you injured?" the woman asked.

Carrie took a shaky breath. "A little. Not bad."

The woman's kind voice helped her relax as she asked questions, and Carrie took stock of her injuries. The blood on her face still dripped, but not so much it worried her. Her legs were fine, not trapped or damaged. In fact, only her wrist and face seemed to be the problem.

And it wasn't bad enough she'd need an ambulance. She looked at the car she'd hit, hoping no one had been in the passenger side. It looked empty, and the guy still standing and examining his car and hers — scowling at her every few minutes — seemed to be healthy and free of injury.

The 911 dispatcher's voice pulled her back to the moment. "The officer has just arrived. Do you see him?"

"Yes," Carrie said.

"There will be an ambulance there shortly to evaluate things."

After making sure Carrie was okay to hang up and that the officer was indeed there, the dispatcher ended the call. She peeked out the windshield to see her car wouldn't be driving away from this. She'd have to call her roommate, Abby, to come get her. *I hope she's not lost in her meditation.*

"Hey, Abby," Carrie said as the girl answered the phone. "I need a favor. Can you come get me? I crashed my car." Carrie sighed as Abby asked a million questions and tried to calm her down and answer them as best as possible. "I'm okay, but I don't think the car is at all. I hurt my wrist and might need a ride to the hospital, but I don't need an ambulance. No, I'm sure. But I'd appreciate it if you could come get me."

When she hung up, she wondered if she should call Mr. Carlson and let him know she'd be late, or if she should take the day off. He would understand. Besides, today wasn't an overly busy day. They'd be meeting with an entrepreneur who wanted some advice on how to get the word out on his non-profit, and she had planned to update the accounts.

She could probably go in after she got her wrist checked out. The throbbing had increased, and the wrist itself looked swollen.

The police officer approached the cars before she could call her boss, followed closely by the guy she'd hit. Carrie took a slow breath to calm her nerves and face the men. She didn't know how this had even happened. She hadn't been distracted, or texting — or anything. She could have sworn the light was green.

After grabbing her purse, she reached for the door with her left hand out of habit and hissed in pain when she jarred her wrist. She stretched her other hand across her body and pulled on the handle to open the door. The fresh air helped her breathe better, and she should have opened it sooner, but she hadn't wanted to talk to the man alone, with him looking that angry.

Hopefully, things would go smoothly. She could exchange insurance information, get the inevitable ticket, and never have to see the guy again. With the narrowed eyes and judging expression on his face, she didn't want to ever speak to him if she didn't have to.

***

Oh great. I've been hit by a real live Barbie. Bryce looked at the tall, shapely blonde as she climbed out of the car. Her skirt hugged her curves, and her light pink blouse accentuated her hourglass figure. Long hair fell loosely over her shoulder, framing her face. The only flaw about her was the cut on her cheekbone where blood trickled down. He reached in his pocket for his handkerchief and passed it to her without saying a word.

Her eyes widened, and she hesitated for a moment before taking it carefully from him, as if afraid he'd yank it back.

"Thank you." She dabbed it gently against her face with her right hand while holding the left arm protectively close to her stomach. *Is she injured more than just the cut?*

The officer approached, assessing the situation. "Sir, please return to your car. I'll be with you in a moment."

Bryce nodded, reluctant to leave, wanting to make sure the woman admitted to running the red light, but since their cars were entwined in an odd embrace, he would probably be able to hear what she said.

"Are you injured, miss?" the officer asked.

Bryce listened as the woman's melodic voice, deeper than he'd expected it would be, described the pain in her wrist. He couldn't take his eyes off her, but the more he watched her smile at the officer and the way she moved her body as if leaning into the man, he knew she was one of *those* types.

He'd been married to one of *them* once, and he never wanted to be with another like her for as long as

8

he lived. Besides, she looked young, probably early twenties at the most. Way too young for him, even if he were looking again.

He had too much on his plate for the moment to even consider dating. Besides, meeting at the scene of a car accident wasn't the way to build any kind of relationship.

As he waited for the officer to finish with the woman — who he thought had said her name was Carrie — he pulled his phone out to contact the company he had an appointment with in a few hours. They would need to reschedule. His car wouldn't be drivable. And though he wasn't injured at all, this mess would take some time to resolve.

He ground his teeth together in frustration that the opening of his community-outreach program might be delayed now.

At least she hadn't been texting. When he'd approached her car after she hit him, she'd seemed dazed and disoriented, but there was no indication she'd been on the phone.

After the officer got her information and statement, he joined Bryce for his. Another officer got statements from any witnesses who'd stuck around long enough to help while a third officer took care of traffic. The ambulance slid through the mess of backed up cars, and an EMT soon moved over to Carrie. She allowed him to check her, but from what Bryce could tell, she didn't seem to think it would be necessary to be transported by ambulance.

Bryce filled out his report, explaining how he'd been waiting at the stoplight for it to turn green. A car had rushed through on the yellow just as it turned red, but the intersection was clear before he moved forward. What possessed the woman to run the light that long after it had changed, he didn't know. Just a dumb blonde that didn't know how to drive.

He looked over at her as she spoke with the EMTs and frowned again at the way she flirted and teased the men there as she sat on the back bumper of the ambulance. This woman was unbelievable. Either she really wasn't in pain and just faking her injury, or she was such a player she didn't know when to show discretion in her flirting.

A dark-haired girl rushed through the circle of bystanders and made her way over to Carrie. She wrapped her in a hug and checked her over. "Carrie, you scared me to death. I'm so glad to see you standing." The girl glanced at the EMTs. "Is she okay?"

Carrie adjusted her arm trying to find a more comfortable position. "I've got a possible broken wrist. But it'll be fine for you to take me to the hospital."

Bryce watched while the other girl comforted Carrie, and he felt a fleeting moment of loneliness.

There was no need for him to call anyone, and he didn't need assistance, but standing there by himself, filling out the accident report and watching everything else unfold in front of him as if he weren't actually a part of it — though he was smack dab in the center of it all — was a confusing emotion.

He didn't need anyone, especially someone like *Barbie* over there, but for a brief moment, he almost wished he could be fussed over and cared about.

Chapter Two

*C*arrie read over the accident report as Abby drove her to the hospital. The guy she'd hit, Bryce Thomson, lived on the other side of town, in the area where the houses cost twice as much as the ones less than a mile away. It was obvious he had money, given the type of car she'd smashed. That would raise her insurance rates. Good thing he wasn't injured, and she hoped he wouldn't come back later, claiming injury.

She had seen enough of him to know he was wealthy and used to getting his way. She hoped this could all go away quickly and with as little annoyance as possible. Mr. Carlson had told her to go ahead and take the day off, and if she wasn't feeling well enough to come in on Monday to let him know, and that he could cover things just fine.

The ER wasn't swamped, but since she hadn't arrived by ambulance, they took their sweet time before calling her back to check her wrist so she cradled it against her stomach and hoped the over-the-counter-pain-pills she'd taken would help. At least the cold pack the EMT gave her helped a little.

By the time she got home, sporting a pink fiberglass cast on the small wrist fracture and some skin glue to hold the cut on her cheek together, she was exhausted. She broke her pill in half, not wanting to feel completely drugged, but needing to take the edge off the pain, and climbed into her bed. Tomorrow she'd figure out what to do for temporary transportation. Her brother, Shane, would probably let her borrow one of his cars, but she'd rather not deal with him about something like that. Some clause in her car insurance policy must exist that would allow her a rental while her car was in the shop. Or, if the insurance adjuster determined it was totaled beyond worth of repair, she would have to look into a replacement.

Adulting was hard, and she wished for a moment she didn't have to do this on her own.

Maybe Abby would drop her off at work. Or she could see if anyone from the office lived close enough to give her a ride. She texted her younger brother, Eric, who was hopefully at school to let him know she wouldn't be surfing with him in the morning and to go with his buddies anyway. She wouldn't be getting in the ocean for more than six weeks.

As the drugs kicked in, Carrie closed her eyes, surprised when the image of Bryce Thomson came to mind. She still had the handkerchief he'd given her to wipe her bloody face. *Who carries actual linen handkerchiefs anymore?* And though he probably had a lot of the hankies, she wondered if she should scrub the blood out of it and mail it back to him, or keep it. She didn't want to ever run into the guy again, but she wished she could have met him under different circumstances. He was handsome in the classic-British-gentleman kind of way. Someone you couldn't help sighing over. At least when he wasn't chewing you out for smashing into his car.

***

Bryce wasn't in pain, really, but he did feel a little stiff as the day wore on. The added stress of getting his car towed to the shop and going home to get one of his other vehicles wasn't too bad, but he was glad the workday was over. He'd need to do a couple of extra things over the weekend. If he worked smart, he could still get the community youth outreach program in the works.

He already had the building, and the permits from the city to do it. He'd hired someone to be in charge of getting volunteer artists and sculptors to mentor the youth who'd be coming for help. He wished he could have gotten the ball rolling with the marketing firm willing to donate some service hours to help get the word out about the program. With the meeting rescheduled for Monday, he would have to move a few things around.

Yet, try as he might, he couldn't focus on everything on his list. A minor ache would remind him of the accident, which, in turn, reminded him of Carrie Winters and his emotions would betray him.

He shouldn't be attracted to her; in fact, she hadn't even spoken to him besides the whispered thank-you for the handkerchief or even apologized for causing the accident. Though she was a total and complete flirt, he still couldn't get her out of his mind. When she had met his eyes after taking his handkerchief, something deep inside the blue irises made him long to look into them forever. She'd seemed almost afraid of him yet had easily chatted with the police officer and EMTs.

Yes, he needed to stay far away from that woman. And, if there were any issues in regard to the accident, he'd let the insurance company and their lawyers take care of them.

*****

Carrie drove extra carefully to work on Monday morning in the rental the insurance company had helped her get. It would be a few days until they completed the paperwork enough for her to get a replacement for her totaled vehicle. As she approached the intersection, she slowed down, even though she was positive the light was green this time. When she'd discussed the accident with the officer on Friday morning, she'd told him the light had looked green, and he'd pointed out how the sunlight at that time of day must have been right on the green, making it glow or reflect enough to appear lit.

She passed the intersection and thought again of Bryce Thomson standing over her window with such anger. She felt more than foolish for having caused the accident, but it was an honest mistake. One she would be sure to avoid in the future.

It took some effort to force him out of her mind, but by the time she pulled into Carlson Ad Agency's area of the parking garage under the office building, Bryce Thomson was no longer her concern. Instead, she prepared to face her day and take care of the accounts. Madison Perry-Koholohini had trained her well, and it was nice to have a specific place to work instead of being the floating intern learning the ins and outs of an ad agency.

While dressing that morning, she'd had second thoughts about picking the neon pink cast, but she'd never had a cast before and thought she might as well go all out. At least she hadn't picked green. And the white would have become grimy-looking pretty quickly.

Eric had been excited to get his hands on her cast as soon as he got home from school. He'd doodled fancy designs all over it, telling her he couldn't resist a blank canvas. At least he wasn't spray-painting buildings anymore. *The kid has all sorts of talent, but if he doesn't focus on school a little more and ease up on his art, he might not graduate.* He would need to get a good job to support himself. She didn't want him to have to go live with their older brother, Shane, and their dad definitely wasn't parenting material, since he was in prison on drug charges.

She'd have to mull it over, see if there was something she could do to help him.

When she reached the office and got off the elevator, she wasn't surprised to see everyone come check on her and ask how she was after the accident. Even Mr. Carlson stepped out of his office and waved her over.

"Glad you're doing well. You had us worried."

"Thanks, Mr. Carlson," Carrie said. "I'm glad it wasn't serious. Though the car didn't make it."

"That's too bad," Mr. Carlson said. "How's your hand?"

Carrie lifted her cast. "There was a small break in the wrist, but it should heal quickly. The cast will be on for six to eight weeks, but my fingers are still usable. I won't have any issues with the computer at all. I'm sorry about missing Friday. I hope your meeting with the entrepreneur went well.

"He had to cancel, apparently he had some car issues or something. Didn't really explain. But we've rescheduled for today at eleven. Will you be able to make it? I think it would be good to have your input. We'll be volunteering our time since this is a non-profit student outreach."

"Yes, I'll be there." Carrie answered a few questions from some of the other employees on her way into her new office then got to work. She had a few hours before eleven and thought she could make a big dent in her client accounts' list.

Though she could type, her hand ached, and she found she used her good hand more than usual, slowing her down a little. She took a quick break and pulled out a couple of over-the-counter pain pills. The doctor said it would ache for a few days, but she hoped it wouldn't interfere much.

In the few hours before eleven, she finished up the current account, sent a couple of emails, billed a few of the clients, and scheduled an appointment for a casting call. The holidays were fast approaching and they'd be getting busier by the day, but she was excited to see Carlson's ideas. She gathered her laptop to join Mr. Carlson in the conference room. As she exited her office, she saw someone who apparently had just gotten off the elevator. She smiled automatically, then when the familiar face registered, the smile slipped from her lips.

"Bryce Thomson?" She narrowed her eyes at the man. *How dare he come to my office? What gives him the right to approach me?* Their insurance companies should take care of things. She would love to file harassment charges against the jerk. "What are you doing here?" she asked. "How did you find my place of work?"

Bryce stopped short and stared at her as if he couldn't believe his eyes. "*Miss* Winters?"

Carrie opened her mouth, annoyed that he stressed the *Miss* part of the name like he was talking about a child. "What gives you the right to harass me, Mr. Thomson? I would never pester you at your work."

He pressed his lips together and stared down at her as if he were irritated, and Carrie's annoyance rose. She racked her brain for something scathing to say, but before she could speak, she heard Mr. Carlson's voice from behind.

"Mr. Thomson, thank you for coming. I see you've met my account manager, Ms. Winters. She'll be sitting in on our consultation."

Carrie felt the blood leave her face, and she closed her eyes, wishing to disappear right there. Of course he would be a client. And she'd just shoved her foot as far into her mouth as humanly possible. As Mr. Thomson turned away from her and focused his attention on Mr. Carlson, she immediately felt dismissed and shunned like she had always felt with her father.

She followed meekly behind, dreading the next hour. In fact, she would have much rather crashed her car again instead of heading toward this wreck.

Chapter Three

*B*ryce chuckled. Carrie would be lucky to keep her job if she didn't grow up soon. She wasn't very professional and would certainly struggle in the workforce if she didn't get over her generation's attitude of entitlement. In his experience, anyone fresh out of college was barely worth an interaction, and the teens today were even worse. He wanted to reach some of them through his art program early enough to help improve them before their entire generation was ruined.

They didn't have as much of a problem as some of the larger cities, but he wanted to do something to keep the youth off the streets and out of trouble. Doing something with the arts would be a good start, and if things worked out well with this endeavor, he'd love to start some theater options. Schools didn't do enough with music and theater or art, so he'd do his best to introduce them to it.

If only more people would get involved. Mr. Carlson had been a friend of his father's and had been highly thought of by his old man before he passed away. It didn't take much to convince Mr. Carlson to donate his time and expertise. Bryce would pay for any of the ads but wouldn't be billed for any of these consultations or brainstorming sessions. He couldn't wait to pick Mr. Carlson's brain for ideas to bring his plan to fruition.

In return, it would be good publicity on their part, and Mr. Carlson understood the importance of outreach programs. He'd shared his experience with his own nephew, who'd struggled as a teen and managed to turn his life around through a program like the one Bryce had in mind.

Mr. Carlson chatted as they walked down the hall, asking questions about Bryce's business and how things had gone after he took over his grandfather's art gallery. Bryce answered easily, but was very aware of Carrie following behind. At least she hadn't said anything more. Mr. Carlson didn't need to know Carrie was the reason he'd had to cancel on Friday. Unless she brought it up, it wasn't important enough to mention.

Bryce didn't worry about working with Carlson's agency or Ms. Winters. The insurance could handle things, and he'd be a professional, even if she couldn't. It wasn't like he'd be forced to interact with her much. Mr. Carlson would be the brains of the planning session. Carrie would most likely act as the secretary or note taker.

Bryce followed Mr. Carlson to the head of the table in the spacious conference room. Carrie walked around the other side of the table and sat in the chair next to Mr. Carlson, putting her directly across from Bryce. He looked at her as she sat down, and the bright pink cast caught his eye. He hadn't noticed the broken arm at first because the fire in her eyes when she first recognized him had claimed all his attention.

A flesh-colored bandage covered the cut on her cheek, and she had a faint hint of bruising around her eyes and the bridge of her nose. She must have been wearing glasses. He was actually impressed she'd returned to work this soon after the accident. Most kids her age would have milked the accident for all it was worth and taken days — if not a week — off work.

He watched her from the corner of his eye, trying not to bring attention to the fact he was aware of her. Mr. Carlson asked him to explain his plans and lay out his ideas for the Carlson Agency to build from. Carrie opened her laptop and started typing as Bryce explained his vision for the community arts outreach program.

He couldn't help noticing she seemed interested in the idea, and as he watched her type, his eyes went to the cast on her left wrist, noticing for the first time the intricate design drawn on it with a marker. Had she doodled that herself? If so, maybe she would know some volunteers to give their time. He wasn't sure if he wanted to ask her to participate, not with how their acquaintance had begun, but perhaps he could get some referrals from her.

As he wrapped up his plans, Mr. Carlson nodded. "I think it's a great idea. You've got a good start on ways to get the news out, but we can do a lot more with some well-placed ads on some city buses, park benches, and such. We can also do a lot with social media. It's ever–changing, and things that worked months ago are not as effective, but Carrie has a good feel for what will work. She can come up with some good ideas and help us reach your target demographic."

Carrie nodded and continued taking notes, never looking toward Bryce. Mr. Carlson carried on. "We'll do some focused plans to the schools and sports communities. And reaching parents is still a good option. Many are looking for things to get their kids involved to keep them from getting into trouble."

They discussed different options and plans for another ten minutes, then Mr. Carlson asked Bryce what his budget was.

"I don't want to overextend ourselves. The outreach program hasn't fully started yet. We have the groundwork done, and the basic architecture of the program is almost finalized. I've received commitments from a handful of artists and sculptors who are dying for a chance to get their names out there. Many are highly talented. The city has agreed to let us advertise on a few of the buses and bus stops *without* charge as an initial push to get the program going, so that won't cost."

"Social media won't cost you anything either," Carrie said. "Unless you need to hire someone to do the initial buzz and work on creating a trending topic. If you've got some volunteers — or yourself — who could keep tabs on that for the first couple of weeks, it's not something that will cost you anything."

"Right," Mr. Carlson agreed. "And unless you want to pay for some localized ad space on a few of the hotter social media outlets, you could get some of your big names and artists to post updates and tweets about this."

Bryce nodded. He hadn't thought much about the power of social media, or how widespread and relatively free it was. "Sounds great. I might be able to get someone to cover that for me. If not, do you know someone I could hire?"

Mr. Carlson smiled. "Find any college student and offer to pay them a couple hundred bucks to set it up."

Bryce nearly rolled his eyes at the suggestion. He didn't think that would be much help. He wanted someone he could trust. "I'll find someone," Bryce said. A few of the artists had to have contacts with people who could help spread the word.

They continued discussing what type of paid advertising would get him the best exposure for the least amount of money. He could fund a lot of it on his own. The inheritance from his maternal grandfather made him independently wealthy, but he didn't want to cover all the costs. His art gallery was more important anyway. For now. He wanted to do something to help teens and bring a little more culture into the city.

***

Carrie watched as Mr. Thomson and Mr. Carlson chatted about the program and wondered how she could get Eric involved in it. And the social media stuff would be easy enough. Maybe she could volunteer to do it. It wouldn't take much time, and she could post occasionally, even while at work.

As they wrapped up the meeting, and Mr. Thomson shook Mr. Carlson's hand, she finished jotting down their ideas then followed them out. She studied Bryce, wondering how old he was. He talked easily with Mr. Carlson, but since they had mentioned Bryce's late father, she knew he was quite a few years younger than Mr. Carlson's late fifties.

Yet given the few comments he'd made, it seemed he thought teens and people in their early twenties were like a whole different generation of people. But he couldn't be much older than early thirties. His face looked young without any sort of wrinkles. His dark hair had no sign of gray or silver at the temples, and the tailored suit fit him well, indicating a fit and trim body beneath it.

She forced her eyes away from his physique, knowing she should stay far away from him that way. Given the accident, he wouldn't take kindly to her flirting with him. Would probably think she was trying to get out of any of the issues with the insurance. And, hearing him talk about his business and his unlimited funds, she didn't want to make him think she was after him for money.

"I've got a small opening tomorrow. You can come back in, and we can show you some of the proposals we'll create for your ads," Mr. Carlson said. "Then you and Ms. Winters can work on some of the social media ideas when I have to leave for my other appointments."

"Thank you for your time, Howard," Mr. Thomson said. "I can't imagine trying to get something like this running all on my own."

"That's why we're here," Mr. Carlson said.

Mr. Thomson turned to Carrie and offered his hand. "Thank you for your assistance. I look forward to seeing your ideas tomorrow."

Carrie extended her hand and placed it in his. He shook it gently then turned away. She was surprised he had never mentioned anything about the accident or even brought it up to Mr. Carlson that they'd met before.

His behavior impressed her, and she hoped they'd be able to work together well. Especially since they would be meeting more often as this outreach program got underway.

Chapter Four

A few days later, Carrie looked at Mr. Thomson sitting across the conference table. The fact that he'd been impressed with all the ad spots for the local papers and news outlets, in addition to the posters that would be placed around the city, was a relief. He'd suggested a few changes, but the things he did point out proved he was astute and on top of things. Yet when Mr. Carlson excused himself and left Carrie to go over the different options of social media and website ideas, Mr. Thomson looked lost.

"These sites look like a bunch of pictures of vain kids just posting proof of their lack of maturity. How am I supposed to use something like this to catch the attention of kids who are too self-absorbed to see anything besides themselves?"

Carrie blinked at the callous comment, but instead of calling him on it, she decided to stay more professional. "It's really not that difficult, Mr. Thomson," Carrie said. "There are people who are looking for things to do. If you use the right hashtags and phrases, you can put yourself out in front of thousands of people who would be interested in what you're offering."

Carrie pulled out her phone and did a search for a few of the artists on his list of mentors. "If you check out some of their websites, Twitter accounts and the like, you'll see they do a lot of self-publicity in the form of providing interesting topics, as well as showing some samples of their work. Nowhere do they say *Buy my stuff*, but because they are interesting and engaging, it pulls the customers to them."

She leaned back and looked at Mr. Thomson. He tilted his head. "So what do I do with that? Get myself some of those accounts and tell people to come to the grand opening and sign up?"

"More or less, but unless you have a little more charm and a lot less intimidation tucked in your sleeves, you'll need to approach it in a different way."

Bryce scowled at Carrie, and she hoped she hadn't just overstepped her boundaries. "Intimidation?" he asked.

Carrie sighed. "You are trying to sell yourself, at least to the point where you will get people to donate their time and money as well as send their children to your program, but the way you dress, for example, or the way you talk about the youth you're trying to help says the opposite of what you want." Carrie could see in his eyes he was trying to take it all in. "I'm telling you this as an advertising consultant. Take what you will." She pointed at his suit and his briefcase on the table. "In a situation like this, your suit is fine, but you put off a vibe of a man who doesn't want anything to do with teens. If I met you on the street with the look you're giving me right now, and then you told me to sign up for your program, it wouldn't matter what you offered me. I'd steer clear of you."

"I didn't realize I gave that impression."

Carrie shrugged. "Not many people are aware of the way their body language or behavior appears to others. It's part of what we do, though, so I'm giving you these pointers now. When you hold your open house, where you'll be speaking with the parents and the school teachers and others with a vested interest in the youth, you'll want to be inviting. Let them know they can safely trust you to mold their youth."

"But I won't be working directly with the kids myself. I'm just setting everything up."

"It doesn't matter. If you are the man in charge, the backbone of this endeavor, people will be coming to you for answers." Carrie placed her hands on the table and looked him up and down. "The scowls will have to go, but I'm not saying you have to completely change your personality. Don't smile if you don't want to, but try to at least look pleasant and open, Mr. Thomson."

"You can call me Bryce," he said as if trying to reform then rearranged his face into a less austere expression.

Carrie smiled, hoping to encourage him.

"Besides my lack of personal appeal, what kinds of things do I need to do for the social media advertising? I'd like to get things underway. The open house is less than a month away, and we need to get things started."

Carrie nodded. "I've written a list of things you could post — also shown it on a timeline. You'll want to post something daily on these sites, hourly on some of these others, and there are a few you could do a couple of times a day. Also, if you can get other people to share, like, retweet, or favorite your information, it will be seen more. And each of the different sites will need a different phrasing. As you'll see, I've listed examples here."

Carrie looked up at Bryce, and his eyes were wide with a hint of panic in them. She sighed, knowing it would be too much for him to take on right now. "You know what, Mr. Thomson, just let me get these going. Consider it part of the consultation with Mr. Carlson."

Bryce smiled, his relief was apparent. "I appreciate it."

"No worries. I think your program is a good idea, and I'd like to do what I can to make sure it succeeds."

Bryce gathered his paperwork and placed it in his briefcase. "Is there anything I need to do specifically with this social media stuff, or do you have it all?"

"I will need to contact you and find out particulars. I'll also run the ideas by you if you'd like. Do you have a number you prefer me to use?"

Bryce reached into his suit pocket and pulled out a business card. He put a small star next to the bottom number. "This one is my office, but if I'm not there, you can call my personal cell." He wrote in the number and passed the card to her. "But try the office first. Or you can email me. It's on the card."

Bryce pointed at the bottom one, brushing her hand with his finger. His skin was warm and soft, and she stared at the length of the finger, ending with a nicely manicured nail. She briefly wondered if he had them done professionally, or if he clipped them himself, taking special care of his cuticles.

Carrie struggled to control her body's response to his simple touch. "Sounds good." Carrie tucked the card in the folder with his other files, planning to enter the numbers in her phone later.

Bryce stood. "I'll check with you in a day or two, unless you need to contact me sooner." He took a few steps to the door then turned and met her eye. "Are you the one I'll be working with as the ads go through, or is that another person in the office?"

Carrie tapped her pencil on the table a couple of times as she looked at the files. She'd thought she had made some progress with Mr. Thomson, but apparently he still didn't seem to think of her as being worth his time. She would always be the woman who'd ruined his car. "It looks like you're assigned to me — unless you'd prefer someone else, which could be arranged." He'd been polite enough when they met to go over the planning for this event, but now the truth had come out.

Bryce blinked. "Oh, no. No need to reassign my account. You'll do nicely." He turned and left the room, making Carrie wonder if she'd completely misjudged him, or if he was more professional in a business setting than she'd imagined the first time she saw him in Mr. Carlson's office.

Either way, she was excited to work with him, if only for the fact his outreach program was such a wonderful idea.

Chapter Five

"Eric, come on. I think you'd enjoy something like this," Carrie said. The outreach program open house was tonight, and she knew if she got him into the building, he'd be hooked. It had taken some convincing to get him to pause his game, though.

"Really, Carrie. I think I can make my own decisions. Besides, I have some homework to catch up on." He waved the hand not holding the game controller toward his backpack he'd dropped by the front door when he came in.

"You weren't going to do it anyway. This is only a couple hours, and you can still do the homework when you get back. I know the guy in charge. We've been working with Mr. Carlson to get the advertisements going on this. I've heard all his plans to get the local artists and sculptors to come do some one-on-one mentoring. You can look at the different mediums of art and get more involved in it."

Eric shook his head. "I'm not an artist, Carrie."

"You could be." She held up her cast to indicate the designs he'd doodled on it. "Everyone comments on this. And I see your sketches and pictures all over the place. Even the graffiti you got busted for was fascinating. You just need to come up with a better place to show that kind of art."

"Whatever." He paused for a few minutes before asking, "Where is this?"

Carrie gave him the details again, knowing she'd finally convinced him to come. The buzz about this grand opening had been promising, and she wanted to see the results of her efforts. To get Eric there from the beginning would be a huge bonus.

"I guess I can fit it in." Eric didn't even glance at her as he turned the game back on. "I'm just going to finish this level. I'll be ready by six-thirty."

Carrie left the room, knowing her best bet would be to avoid nagging him. He didn't need to get dressed up anyway, but that didn't mean she planned to go in the same clothes she'd worn to work. To her, this was a business event, and she needed to look the part — well-dressed, but not overdone and intimidating.

When she came out of her room, Eric was ready, just as he'd promised.

The drive to the rec center wasn't long, and Carrie stopped her new car in the parking lot of the building Bryce had purchased. She had no doubt he'd make good use of the place, given he'd already filled a handful of the rooms with equipment and materials for artists.

The more she interacted with the guy, the more she realized he was amazing. He planned to open a theater and musical program after he got this one established. She couldn't wait to see where things would go from here.

***

Bryce had decided against his tailored suit since the comment from Carrie made him realize it gave off a more stuffy impression. Though he didn't dislike teens, he honestly didn't know how to interact with them. He was the youngest of his family, didn't have any nieces or nephews anywhere close, and though he wanted to do something for the youth, he was at a loss.

So getting advice and tips from Carrie had helped. He already felt more at ease as the youth and their parents or guardians came to the open house.

His volunteer artists were chatting comfortably with the patrons and explaining how the program would work. A few people approached him, but he mostly observed the interactions going on around him. He needed to hire a personal assistant, someone to talk to the people, to keep him from having to make small talk.

As the thought entered his mind, he spotted Carrie Winters from Carlson's agency standing next to a lanky teen. At first glance, he wondered if he was her date but dismissed the idea immediately. It had to be a friend or a relative with the way they interacted with each other. She pointed out a few things in the area, and the kid nodded then meandered away, peeking into the classrooms as he went.

Carrie also looked around the main entryway and spotted him. Her eyes lit up, doing strange things to his thoughts. She seemed genuinely happy to see him, and he didn't understand why. He hadn't been very friendly when they'd first met and had completely mishandled things. He should never have approached her car and shouted at her. He didn't blame her for chewing him out when he first saw her in Carlson's office. Of course she would have worried he was harassing her. And he'd given her the silent treatment, not even considering her worth his time.

But the more they had interacted during the consultations, the more he realized she had a sharp mind hidden under the long blonde hair twisted in a loose braid and hanging over one shoulder. Her skirt was casual, but very feminine, and flattered her like everything he'd seen her wear.

He tried to force those thoughts from his mind. He did not need a woman in his life, especially one ten years younger. And not one that reminded him of his unfaithful ex. They didn't look anything alike, but her flirtatious nature was something he didn't want to live through again. *Women like that don't stay committed to anyone for long.*

No, he would stay far away from Carrie. Or, at least keep the relationship completely professional, because, as he watched her interact with everyone in the room, looking genuinely happy to be there and making the people around her gravitate toward her, he knew she would be the perfect assistant.

Question is, can I convince her to help? He didn't want to take her away from Carlson. Not with how well she worked there and hearing how Carlson praised her skills as they'd worked on this event. But perhaps he could get her to join him for evenings like this and to help improve his art gallery's events. She'd suggested they hold some amateur artist galas in conjunction with the professional artist who had mentored those youth. They could have an opening night when the artist's work was unveiled and have the other artwork on display farther back in another room. It would help increase local interest since the kids, parents, and neighbors would come to see what their students had done and give the artist more exposure.

Bryce met her eyes again as she looked around the room, apparently searching for someone else —

probably the kid she came in with — and he made a split-second decision. *I will ask her to help me out. She has to say yes.* He wanted her to spend time with him for a reason he couldn't explain. It definitely wasn't because of any interest in her. No, it was a smart business decision. He excelled at those things.

***

Carrie had felt like she'd been watched from the moment she entered the building. She searched the room and found Bryce looking at her. He had taken her suggestion to not overdress for the occasion and looked even better in his casual blazer and trousers than she'd expected. Nothing could compare to him in his tailored suits, but they made him look so uptight and unapproachable. At least he had toned things down for the evening.

He still didn't have many people talking with him. A couple of people, including the mayor and the superintendent of the school district had been with him a little earlier, but now he stood alone and watched her. She took a slow breath and headed his way. *Might as well congratulate him on his success.* Mr. Carlson would expect a report on the event since he wasn't able to make it.

As his eyes seemed to follow her every move, she wanted to look away, feeling uncomfortable at his scrutiny, but forced herself to keep her gaze locked on him. She would not let Bryce intimidate her. *Who cares if he is rich and connected and has people doing exactly what he wants?*

His eyes didn't look as dark and brooding as they often had, and she wasn't sure if she was relieved or concerned about the look he'd actually given her. It wasn't really admiration or anything to indicate he thought her attractive. She'd been looked at that way most of her life, and someone not falling for her looks was both refreshing and disconcerting.

He smiled as she neared, but it didn't quite reach his eyes. No, it was more polite than anything.

Carrie relaxed a little. "Congratulations, Mr. Thomson. It looks like you'll have lots of kids signing up for the program. I've already seen a couple dozen applications turned in."

"That is an excellent start. And we're only into the evening an hour. I appreciate all the hard work you put into this."

Carrie nodded. "I'm glad I got to be a part of it. It's a great idea. In fact, I brought my brother here tonight. He's an artist at heart but just needs to channel it better. I think this will be perfect for him."

"I'm glad," Bryce said. He paused and looked around the room.

Carrie wondered if she should excuse herself to go talk to a couple of the artists and catch up with Eric, but she didn't want to seem rude for leaving immediately. *Maybe a little more small talk first, then I can leave.*

"Mayor Larsen looked impressed with the turn out. And this building is perfect for your plans. In fact, I think using this old rec center is a great idea. You've got enough room in the back to start your theater and music program once this is up and running."

"That was my plan."

"If you need any help with marketing or building up buzz for that once you get started, please don't hesitate to come to Carlson's. Of course, I'm sure you and Mr. Carlson have discussed things already, but I would love to be a part of it."

Bryce smiled, and Carrie thought he should do that more often.

"It's funny you should mention that, because I have a proposition for you. I don't want to take you from Mr. Carlson, but I would like to know if I could interest you in a part-time job working with me on these types of events in the evenings a few times a month."

Carrie looked at Bryce, wondering when his low opinion of her had changed. From all their interactions, she had been under the impression he thought her too young and inexperienced to know anything about his plans or business. Yet here he was, asking her to help out.

"I'm sure Mr. Carlson could assist you in anything you need. And as always, I'm there to help the agency and our clients any way I can."

Bryce nodded. "I will keep in close communication with Howard, of course, but this would be aside from that. I want to hold some events where these amateur artists will display their works at the same time their mentor artist is having their gallery displays. So every month, we'll have an open house at my gallery. I'll need someone with your ability to schmooze and charm everyone in the room, to play hostess. I'm good with plans, numbers, and convincing people to do what I want, but I don't have your social skills. With the two of us together, I think we could get this outreach program off to a fantastic start and bring in more culture to the community."

Carrie listened to the man explain his plan, but when he'd finished, she wasn't sure what to say. Of course she'd love to work with him on this project. She thought the plan was genius, but she wasn't sure if the two of them should work so closely. He did things to her heart and emotions she didn't usually feel for anyone else.

"I'm not sure that would be a good idea," Carrie said after a few minutes. "I don't know if I could commit to your schedule, not with the extra workload I've recently taken on at Carlson's."

Bryce studied her for a moment. "Suit yourself, but I won't beg."

He turned around, and Carrie stared at him with her mouth open. She reached out and turned him back around to face her before he could walk away. The surprise in his eyes distracted her for a moment, but she would not let him bully her into accepting this offer by pouting like a child.

"Excuse me, Mr. Thomson, but I wasn't trying to make you beg. I don't work that way. I am busy and do have a life outside the office. Unless you can give me more specifics and let me have time to think this over, I'll have to say no. From what I know of you, you're a pretty demanding person, and if I commit to something, I do it." She crossed her arms over her chest and regretted it when the stiff cast banged into her other arm. It lessened the severity of her gesture. She took a slow breath and met his eyes. "Feel free to write up a proposal like you do with all your other projects and let me know. You know where to find me."

Carrie turned around and moved away before he could stop her. *The nerve of the man.* She would love to work with him on some of these projects, but after watching him get his way with anyone they'd worked with to get this running right now, she wasn't going to let him walk all over her. She would set her limits and expect him to abide by them. No way would she turn into his personal assistant and be at his beck and call. She knew he had money, but he was shrewd and tightfisted with his funds. The fact they had gotten donations and grants for all the initial supplies and equipment for this outreach program proved he could get what he wanted.

It just won't be me.

***

Bryce watched Carrie walk away and felt equally annoyed and impressed. He would write up a proposal and present it to her. He was sure he could convince her to work for him. He'd pay her of course, but the fact that she didn't jump at his offer was impressive. Most women who knew of his wealth were more than willing to do anything he wanted in hopes of favors or of at least trying to get a date.

He never encouraged women to throw themselves at him, yet they did it anyway. The combination of his looks and money were enough to override his austere persona. Yet Carrie was a different sort all together. Very different from the Barbie-type he'd initially pegged her as. Her beauty was completely natural and only slightly enhanced with just the right amount of makeup. She dressed nice, without overdoing it, and though he could never be sure, he thought her figure was all-natural, with no surgical enhancements. He'd seen enough of those in Southern California to spot the fakes easily enough.

He watched her backside as she walked away from him and felt like a dirty old man. She was too young for him, yet he hated to admit he didn't care. He wanted to get to know her better, to spend time with her. Not date her or get too close that way, but he loved her upbeat personality as well as her no-nonsense kind of attitude.

The approach of the arts alliance director cut his study of the mesmerizing woman short. As she congratulated him on a successful launch, he kept Carrie in sight for as long as possible.

Eventually she met up with her brother and some other man, obviously not her brother by the overly friendly hug she gave him.

He would do well to remember what a flirt she was. He would work with her and use her talents to further his plans for this outreach program, but he would keep his heart locked away. No one would have a chance to stomp on it again.

Chapter Six

*C*arrie typed up a report for a client and reflected on the night before. Eric hadn't stopped talking about what a cool project it was and how excited he was to participate. He'd talked with a guy who did spray-paint art on the side, who showed him a few of his pieces, and Eric was excited to try it.

From what Carrie knew of Bryce's plan, he had picked artists and matched them with mentors who would not only assist them in their art, but would also be the type to encourage them to make good life choices. One artist was a recovering addict. Another artist had survived abuse as a child. One was a former gang member who had successfully freed himself from that environment and made a new life.

Eric wasn't in a lot of trouble yet, but if he kept going down the path he'd started on, things would get bad fast. Carrie was relieved to know at least now he had some different options.

A knock on her door brought her head up, and

she caught herself staring into Bryce's smoky hazel eyes. Though he wore a suit, he didn't look overly stuffy standing in her doorway. In fact, she thought he added a lot to her decor and wished, for a moment, she had a reason to have him in her office all the time.

"Can I come in?" Bryce asked.

Carrie nodded, not sure she could trust herself to speak. She had been rude to him again last night when he'd asked her to volunteer at the events. She'd wanted to say yes, but with having to make payments to cover the cost of the replacement car not covered by the insurance and still having enough for rent, she didn't want to risk losing her job with Carlson.

"I have the proposal you asked for last night."

Carried raised her eyebrow. "Proposal?"

Bryce lifted a manila envelope. "The hours and times you wanted to know, as well as the proposed income."

"Income?" Carrie asked. "This isn't a volunteer position you indicated?"

"Did you think I meant for you to do it pro bono?" Bryce's eyes sparkled and looked as if something clicked inside. Was he making judgments about her? Confusion washed over Carrie, and she felt foolish for the assumption.

"Well, yes. All of your artists and mentors were doing this for free. You are very careful about your expenditures and have gotten donations or exemptions from every business you've contacted. Even Mr. Carlson is doing this for free."

Bryce nodded. "A valid assumption, given your observations. I should have been clearer. I would like to hire you as my assistant for some of these extra events. You will still have time to work with Mr. Carlson. I would never dream of stealing you from him. You are good at what you do, and I don't want to lose my connection to Carlson by this. From what I have gathered by working with you, I think you have the organizational skills to allow you to do a few extra hours a week with an occasional evening event a few times a month."

He passed her the folder and waited for her to open it. Carrie studied him for a moment longer, not sure what to think of the man. She had always been able to read people before, but every assumption she'd made of this guy had proven wrong.

He raised a brow again and looked at the folder in her hands. She turned her attention to it and undid the clasp. As she slid the papers out, her eye focused on the dollar amount, and she did a double take. The hourly rate was higher than her hourly rate with Carlson. If she worked a few hours a week doing the social media marketing as she'd begun doing on this outreach program, and added a few of the gallery events as hostess and marketing person, she could almost raise her income by half.

She forced herself not to look at Mr. Thomson. She would look like a fool or just interested in the money if she immediately accepted the offer. She set the papers down on her desk and read each word from the top to the bottom. Nodding at some of the things she liked and making notes next to where she'd like clarification.

"This is a decent proposal, Mr. Thomson. I will have to speak with Mr. Carlson to make sure he's okay with me taking on this extra load. My first loyalty goes to Carlson Ad Agency, of course, but I think this sounds doable."

Bryce nodded. "I'm glad. When will you let me know?"

"Tomorrow?"

Bryce took a slow breath, but nodded. She glanced back down at the list of proposed times and events and didn't see one that would need her attention immediately. His next gala wasn't for two weeks, but if she did take on this project, two weeks would be enough time to get the word out. Barely.

"Thank you, Ms. Winters. I look forward to hearing from you." He stepped back, making her feel lonely, even though he was only a couple of feet away. His scent lingered, and she wished she knew what cologne he wore so she could buy some and spritz her entire office and apartment with it.

"Thank you, Mr. Thomson," Carrie said after she shook herself out of the confusion she felt. "I'll let you know soon."

"I appreciate it. I do hope you accept. I think you'd help this outreach program get where we need it to be."

Carrie smiled. "Thank you." She watched as he left and wondered what she could say to Mr. Carlson to make sure he didn't have a problem with her taking on this extra job. She would have to ease up a little on her social life, but things had cooled down fast after her breakup with her boyfriend from college, not long after starting work at the agency.

She finished working on the stuff on her workload, then before her lunch break, she gathered up the papers from Mr. Thomson. She wanted to do this job. So much. And not just for the extra income. It would be so much fun to be involved with the artists in the community and then make contacts with people in theater. If they could turn the lives of kids like Eric around, it would be well worth her time, even if she never got paid a dime.

Carrie approached Mr. Carlson's office. His secretary smiled, and Carrie glanced at the open door. "Is Mr. Carlson free?"

"He's not in any meetings right now. I think he's free for a bit." She waved her forward. "Just knock."

Carrie took a few steps to the door, and Mr. Carlson caught her eye. He waved her in without her needing to knock. "How can I help you, Ms. Winters?"

"I wanted to talk to you about something. I met with Mr. Thomson last night."

"Oh, right. He told me he wanted to hire you for some things after hours. Assured me it wouldn't interfere with your current workload. I think you'd be great at it. Are you taking the offer?"

Carrie blinked in surprise. Why hadn't Mr. Thomson indicated he'd already talked to Mr. Carlson? Had he done it before he offered her the job, or after he left her office this morning? Either way, it felt like she was being forced into things because of the whims of a man who thought he could buy anything he wanted.

Throw money at it, sweet talk, or bully your way, and it's yours. She'd show him.

Carrie opened her mouth to say she wasn't going to accept the offer, but Mr. Carlson continued talking about how good it would be for her resume. She'd learn skills doing the publicity for Mr. Thomson's gallery that would, in turn, help her move up the ranks in the ad agency. "And because he's no good at social engagements — never has been — he could use some help from someone like you."

Mr. Carlson smiled at Carrie, and she gave a tentative smile back, confused on what to do. Mr. Thomson might have the ability to plan and the connections to run something like this outreach program, but to get it where it could be, he'd need her. But she would let him know exactly where things stood with them. No more going behind her back.

***

Bryce's phone rang, and he pulled it out, not sure who the number belonged to, and hoped it would be Carrie. Instead, it was the representative from her car insurance company. The news wasn't bad, just more hoops to jump through before they'd pay for the damage Carrie had caused. They had never spoken about it after she'd accused him of stalking her and pestering her at work, right after the accident.

He could tell she didn't want to speak about it, and that suited him. He hadn't handled himself the best way, given the fact he'd scared her enough she locked herself in the car until the officer arrived on scene.

He would need to be more of a gentleman in all their other interactions. As he finished answering the agent's questions, he returned to what he'd been working on before. His phone rang again, and he pressed answer.

"Bryce."

"This is Carrie."

Bryce smiled. Finally. They could get to work right away. "Thank you for calling. When are you free to go over the details of when you'll start? I have quite a few events coming up soon I'd like to get a jump on."

Carrie didn't answer for a moment, and he checked his phone to make sure they were still connected.

Finally, her voice came through. "I'm not sure if this will work out, Mr. Thomson. I had called with the intent to ask you a few questions about what would be expected of me, but, apparently, you and Mr. Carlson have already made the decision, assuming I was yours to command. I will not work under those conditions. I don't care what you would pay me. I am not going to be at your beck and call."

Bryce blinked in surprise. He'd offered her an amazing salary for such a short amount of work, and she was turning him down? He was sure her financial situation would be in trouble after the accident and her hospital bills and raised rates.

"Ms. Winters, I am not trying to control you or command you to do anything. I merely thought we would be a good team. Watching you interact with your brother and kids his age at the event the other night, I assumed you would enjoy doing something like this on an intellectual level, not just for the money."

"I am interested in it. The money is a bonus, no denying that. But if I do work for you, I would expect reasonable notice of your plans. I won't show up when you want me, just because you need someone to be your runner. I have something valuable to contribute to the Carlson Ad Agency, as well as to help you, but I won't sacrifice one for the other.

"And, I will be the one to make decisions affecting me. Mr. Carlson is not my father, and you didn't need to go behind my back and ask my boss if it would be okay to hire me. I should have been able to discuss this opportunity on my own, to work out my own terms for this deal."

"I wasn't going behind your back. I respect Howard and wanted to make sure I didn't jeopardize my relationship with him by hiring one of his employees."

Carrie breathed slowly enough he could hear her through the phone. He didn't seem good at reading people, but he was sharp enough to know he'd irritated her. He needed her help. She could take this project a lot farther than he could on his own, but knew he would not beg.

"So tell me your terms?" Bryce asked. "What will it take for you to accept my offer of employment?"

As Carrie began to lay out her requirements, he interrupted her. "Why don't we meet for lunch and go over the details."

Carrie sighed. "See, that right there, Mr. Thomson, is one of the things I can't stand. I was in the middle of speaking, and you talked over the top of me. If you don't learn some basic social skills and have the common decency to listen, we really won't work well. I'm afraid I'm going to have to say no. Thank you for the offer, but it wouldn't work."

She hung up the phone before he had a chance to apologize. *Why is she so upset?* He drummed his fingers on the desk then looked at his watch and made a couple of quick calculations on the likelihood of finding her at Carlson's before she left for the day — if she had even called him from work.

Bryce had her home address on the accident report, but didn't think she'd take too kindly to him going there. If she'd been upset he'd spoken directly to her boss, she would feel highly offended he'd come to her home.

He pushed his projects to the side and headed out to his car. He needed to speak to her in person, where she couldn't hang up on him or cause a scene in public.

As he drove toward Carlson's Ad Agency, he wondered why he even bothered. There had to be other people just as skilled in marketing he could hire as an assistant and hostess for these events.

But why is she the only one I can imagine by my side at the gallery?

Chapter Seven

As soon as Carrie hung up on Bryce Thomson, she regretted it. That money would have come in handy. But she would not be bullied or treated like a second class citizen. She had finally learned how to stand up for herself when she left home to get out of the meddling eye of her older brother, Shane, after her mom remarried and moved away. She would not let some guy who thought he was better than her make her feel bad.

She dove into her assignments and client accounts with renewed vigor. She had an hour until work officially ended, but with her taking time to mull over the job offer from Bryce, she was slightly behind. It was probably a good thing she'd turned him down. She could focus on the work she needed to do here for Mr. Carlson. But as she thought of her boss, she hoped he wouldn't be disappointed in her for not helping Bryce out. They had a history and knew each other well. And Bryce's plans for the community-outreach program would be a benefit to the entire community.

If only he wasn't such a self-centered jerk.

Carrie turned to her phone as it rang, and she recognized the number immediately. Bryce Thomson. She debated for a moment about letting it go to voice mail, but answered it instead. "Carrie Winters."

"Ms. Winters, please don't hang up. I would like to request a meeting with you. Is there a time today or tomorrow you are free?"

Carrie smiled. He was persistent. She had to give him that. And it seemed like he was trying. A refreshing change from the usual phone calls she got from attractive men. He wasn't asking her out. He wanted to hire her. She could listen to him and either work out a deal that would benefit them both or convince him this idea wasn't a good one for either of them.

"I have at least another hour to get caught up here, but after that I'm available." As she said it, she wondered if that made it sound like she was open for a date or had no social life. Then she told herself she didn't care. He wasn't interested in her as a woman, just as an employee, if that.

"Would you be interested in discussing this over dinner?"

"Depends." Carrie wasn't dressed for anywhere fancy, but he also didn't seem to be the kind to splurge on unnecessary things. "Where should I meet you?"

"I could pick you up at Carlson's. I'm on my way, actually. That way you wouldn't have to worry about driving in traffic."

Carrie closed her eyes. *Is he insulting my driving or just clueless?* "No thank you. I'll meet you if you'll give me a location. I'd prefer to have my own car and leave on my own terms."

There was no response for a moment, then Bryce gave her the name of a restaurant nearby, one where she wouldn't feel underdressed. She'd met clients there before for lunch.

"I'll see you there at six," Carrie said.

"I appreciate your time. Thank you, Ms. Winters."

Bryce's voice through the phone sounded professional, but the deepness of his voice added enough sexiness Carrie wished for a moment this wasn't a business meeting until he spoke again.

"I look forward to getting to work right away."

Yup. He still thinks I'll accept the job, and this is all just a formality.

Though it was true, she needed to make sure he didn't think he could have everything he wanted. Even if he was going to employ her, she would not let him boss her around.

***

Carrie entered the restaurant and immediately adjusted her purse over her shoulder.

The maître d' gave a partial smile and raised his brows as if to ask how he could help her.

She smiled in return. "I'm meeting Bryce Thomson."

"Of course. Right this way, Ms. Winters."

Carrie nodded. It didn't surprise her that Bryce had given her name to the front. She followed him through the restaurant to a nice table for two set up in the quieter corner of the room. Bryce stood as she approached and moved around to her chair, then pulled it out in time for her to sit down as they arrived. She worried for a moment she wouldn't know how to sit in it correctly as he scooted the chair forward, but either she wasn't so bad, or he was experienced. As he took his hand off the chair, his finger brushed her arm and sent shivers down her left side and into her cast.

Ugh, I wish I hadn't picked this bright pink cast. It would be another few weeks before they removed it. Most people didn't seem to notice at all, but here in the nice restaurant, she felt a little conspicuous. As if only perfection should be in here. And given the way Mr. Thomson looked, she thought he fit here perfectly.

"I need to apologize up front for anything I might say this evening that offends you. I'm sure you've noticed I don't have the social skills you seem to come by so naturally. I don't mean to sound so demanding or controlling, but I know what I want, and usually, I'm able to get it with little difficulty. You, Ms. Winters, are something I'm not used to."

Carrie raised her eyebrows, but given the fact he'd apologized in advance, she didn't feel offended, just surprised at his bluntness.

"Apology accepted on one condition. You don't take offense at what I might say. I'm not going to sugarcoat things. If you want me to help you with your projects, I'm going to tell you what I like and don't like about how you're doing things. No one should have to be uncomfortable with the people they work with."

Bryce leaned closer over the table. "Are you uncomfortable around me?"

Carrie shrugged. "At times. But I'm used to domineering men who think they can demand things from others. My older brother is that way, not to mention my father. I watched my mom bend over backward to make them happy. But I'm not that way. Never was. I won't tolerate it — from anyone, not even a boss."

"So you'll do things your own way?" Bryce asked. "With no input from your employer?"

"That isn't what I said." Carrie leaned back and clasped her hands together as gracefully as she could with the cast's interference. "I will take your instructions and input and make decisions based on those, but I would never allow you to walk all over me. I don't care if you are rich. I don't want to be miserable just to make money."

"That is good news, because I wouldn't want to pay a miserable, ornery person. I watched you interact seamlessly with so many guests at the open house the other night. With some, it looked like you knew them, but others I'm sure were complete strangers, and every single person you talked to seemed to gravitate back toward you. Like a magnet. Me?" Bryce paused and shook his head. "I repel people. The only ones who ever come to me want something. Over time, I've developed a harder shell to discourage people from begging, but I'm not happy. I want to do something good and valuable with my money. But I don't want to throw it away on a project that won't work because I lack a personality trait you overflow with."

He picked up his glass and took a slow drink, keeping his gaze on her. "Together, we could be a wonderful team. Will you work for me?"

Carrie reached for her drink as well; she needed time to consider. "What about a one-month trial? We both know we have some issues. And, after our rocky start, maybe we shouldn't make any huge commitments. If we can stand to work with each other, we can make it a longer-term proposition."

Bryce nodded. "Sounds fair. I have one exhibit scheduled for a few weeks from today — November eleventh, I believe — and the artist is one of the mentors. She works in watercolors, so I think there would be a few youth who might have some pieces to display. It would start slow, and we can build from there. I have plans for a large event, showcasing a handful of artists for the week after Christmas, but had considered doing it as a New Year's Eve celebration. I wanted to pick your brain about that. Would we have time for some marketing to prepare for it? Would it be the best use of time?"

Carrie considered the possibilities for a moment. *This city has been lacking cultural events. This will be a good way to start things up.*

"I think it has potential."

"I know you said a month, but what if we tried for three months? Let's go to the end of this quarter. If we haven't worked out a good partnership by then, we can dissolve this with no hard feelings."

Carrie took another sip of her drink. She hoped they could part ways amicably. *I'm sure I can be professional about it, but he is demanding. Can I soften him up enough to seem normal?*

"I'll give it a shot. But if you turn into a jerk, I have

no problem quitting. I'll give you two weeks' notice so you can find a replacement, but I won't stay in a bad situation."

Bryce studied her for a minute before replying. "You make me sound like some kind of ogre or monster."

Carrie smiled and fluttered her eyes at him. "If the club fits."

***

Bryce blinked, surprised at her comment. She really didn't have a high opinion of him, and, for some reason, that bothered him. At least she had agreed to give this partnership a go. Their server returned and asked if they were ready to order. For a moment, Bryce considered ordering for her since he knew the best dishes on the menu, but when Carrie looked down at her menu for the first time since arriving, he looked up at the server. "Give us a few minutes, please."

The waiter nodded, and Carrie glanced at Bryce. "I'm surprised you didn't order for me."

Bryce opened his mouth, then closed it before studying her a moment. "I wouldn't dare."

"I see you can be taught. Thank you." She smiled at him then returned her attention to the menu.

He studied her while her eyes were elsewhere and admired her features. Her hair was held back from her face by a jeweled clip, but wispy strands still fell forward. He wondered how soft it was. It looked baby fine, but had body, instead of appearing flat or stringy.

She perused the menu, her green eyes returning to the top after every glance at the bottom. He wondered between which two items she was debating. She looked up, and he glanced away for a moment, feeling embarrassed at being caught staring, but as he picked up his water glass, he met her eyes again.

"Have you decided?"

"Almost," Carrie said. "It's between the fillet mignon and the lobster tails." Her long fingers tapped the menu. "Have you tried either of them?"

"They are both good choices. I'm ordering the lobster myself."

Carrie's gaze returned to the menu, and she tapped the top. "The fillet it is."

Bryce tilted his head to study her, not sure what that meant. *Is she being contrary, or does she want a bite of my lobster?* Not that he had a problem sharing, but he wanted to be prepared if she asked. He tucked away the thought for a moment and signaled the waiter.

"We're ready. I'll have the lobster, and she'll have the fillet." Bryce turned to her.

Carrie nodded and answered the questions the waiter asked. She smiled and made eye contact with the man, and though she seemed comfortable and bold with him, she didn't flirt like she had with the EMTs.

Does she not find him attractive or is she holding back because she's out with me? Not that this is a date. Bryce found himself wondering what it would be like to date her, to be free to take her hand or escort her. When he'd assisted her into the chair, he'd been tempted to trail his hand across her back, and the impulse surprised him. He hadn't wanted to get close to a woman for a long time. The hurt and betrayal of his wife's abandonment had scarred him more than he wanted to admit.

As they waited for their meal to arrive, Carrie made small talk, asking him a few questions about his day. He answered as sparsely as possible, not wanting to bore her. In fact, he wanted to get back to planning the event for his next gallery showcase. But maybe she was testing him, to see if he'd take over the conversation.

He allowed himself to answer more of the questions, and even asked a few of his own. *I can count this as an interview for the job. Having a bit of her background will help.*

"What made you go into marketing and advertising?" Bryce asked.

Carrie shrugged. "I don't know if I ever consciously decided to pursue it. It kind of fell in my lap. I'd gone to college, had a couple of classes where

I enjoyed dealing with computer design. My digital-design professor told me about an internship at an ad agency, and I looked into it. Mr. Carlson was great to work with and allowed me to continue as an intern with an actual paycheck while still in college. I loved it so much I changed my degree to graduate in marketing.

"And you enjoy it still?" Bryce asked.

"I love it. It's wonderful to look at a problem, offer suggestions on how to assist. And, though I'm not doing the actual pitching and creating commercials, I'm still involved in almost every aspect. Working directly with the clients on accounts is good too. It helps me see what's working, what's not."

Bryce listened to her go on about her college days; she talked about her roommate — the same girl who had come to pick her up the day of the accident — and her younger brother. Though he was sure she'd once mentioned an older brother, she didn't talk about him at all.

The more he listened to her, the more he wanted to know and hoped things would work well for their partnership.

Chapter Eight

*C*arrie worked her way down the sidewalk past the shoppers and pedestrians as she headed toward Bryce's outreach-program building. She'd made sure to eat dinner before coming, since she didn't know what to expect. Their dinner last night had turned more to chatting and less about the plans for the outreach, and Carrie was pleasantly surprised at how fun he was to be with when he wasn't bossing her around.

He hadn't revealed much about his past but had indicated he no longer had any family. He'd inherited his grandfather's art gallery, in addition to his wealth, and had increased it by some smart business investments. She wasn't sure, but a couple of his evasive answers made her think he'd been married once. She had never heard of him before, but that didn't mean anything since the city was large, and he wasn't the type to be followed by media sharks curious about playboy images. Mr. Thomson seemed very private, actually, and had only recently started looking into doing something with his money.

Carrie smiled and nodded at the people she passed, and when she reached the entrance to the building, she tried the handle but found it locked. She knocked on the door and waited for a few moments, but no one answered. Carrie pulled out her phone to double check the time then reaffirmed on her calendar that she wasn't late. He was.

She scrolled through her recent calls, searching for his number, pressed send, and waited for him to answer.

"Bryce," he said as he answered the call.

"Mr. Thomson," Carrie said. "I'm here at the outreach building. Will you be here soon?"

"Outreach? No, I am at my office. Isn't that where we decided to meet?"

Carrie shook her head slowly at the misunderstanding. She replayed the conversation at the end of dinner and was sure she hadn't heard him say office. "I don't believe you ever specified your office. In fact, I don't even know where that is. I am here on Casa Blanca Street, standing in front of your door looking mighty strange."

"Ms. Winters, I'm sorry about the mix up. My office is on Vista del Sol, about a mile west."

Carrie turned to the west and then looked down at her shoes. A mile away wasn't much, but she didn't feel like doing it in heels. Besides, she'd be quicker returning to her car and driving to his office. "I'll be there in about fifteen minutes," Carrie said into the phone.

"No, wait," Bryce said. "It makes more sense to meet at the outreach building. We can go over a few of our plans for the next few weeks and get an idea of what we're doing next. Besides, the gallery isn't far from there. We can walk over to it afterward. I'll be there in a few minutes. Are you okay to wait?"

Carrie glanced around the neighborhood. It wasn't a slum, by any means, but there were issues with the street, something that the city would need to take care of soon. The buildings looked run down and boring. *Maybe some of the kids in the program will get involved in the cleanup.* The sun hadn't set yet, so the street lights would be sufficient. "I'll be fine. See you soon." She hung up her phone and studied the area more closely, her mind brimming with ideas on how to get people involved.

When Bryce showed up ten minutes later, she'd written a few things in her phone. She was excited to show him, but not sure what he would think.

He unlocked the door to the building and motioned for her to enter first. She stepped into the dark building, glad the front doors had some glass in them to allow enough light to see. Bryce followed soon behind her and found the light switches along the side wall. He locked the door from the inside, making Carrie feel safe yet nervous to be alone with him.

She didn't worry he'd do anything to her physically. In fact, she was almost sure he'd never touch her other than the proper handshake of business associates. She took a step back when he turned around and headed toward the largest room in the building, the same one they'd used for the artists to display their work for the open house. He didn't seem to notice her discomfort, and she was glad. The last thing she needed was for him to be aware that she wasn't completely comfortable and in control of things.

When he reached the doors to the large room, she took a few steps forward, her heels clicking on the tile floor and echoing in the empty building.

"It was a lucky thing for me this building was available, being so close to my gallery. I think having the programs here where the youth can create projects, then have a few of them showcased in the gallery will allow the youth a sense of accomplishment."

Carrie nodded. "I agree. I think the kids would be ecstatic to find their work in a professional gallery with other artists. It will give them something to work toward." She glanced back toward the front of the building. "However, I'm sure you noticed the neighborhood could do with a little tender loving care."

Bryce nodded. "I've talked to the city about it, but the street here isn't scheduled for repaving for a while."

"That's too bad," Carrie said. "But I had an idea I wanted to run past you." When he turned around to face her, she took out her phone to show him some pictures. "I think if we just did a few touch-ups in the area to enhance the good things about it, we could make a difference without a lot of effort. I figured the youth involved in the program would be interested in helping out. The only thing I would need would be a bit of petty cash to get the paints and the raw materials."

"How much are you thinking?"

Carrie opened her app where she'd taken some notes and went over her guesstimate. As she spoke, he seemed open enough to the idea, so she continued on, getting excited with the details. "And I don't think it would take them long to get it finished. Once I get the approval from the city and talk to the local businesses, I'm sure we could get things underway in no time."

"Are you sure you have the time to do this, as well as help with the gallery exhibit in two weeks?"

Carrie looked at her calendar. Her days would be busy at Carlson's, but she would have every evening open. There were no dates or social events scheduled. "I've already done a lot of the preliminary work for your event on the eleventh. This project will only take a little bit of work from me. I know someone who can help me get this rolling. There is time to get all this done before your next outreach event here in January."

Bryce studied her for a moment, and she met his gaze, wondering what he was thinking. He was hard to read, but this idea excited her, and she would fight for it. Even if it meant she had to wait for a few weeks for the gallery event to end before she could really begin.

"I think it sounds like a great idea. I'll give your information to my accountant. He'll make sure you have some funds to get this started."

Carrie smiled wide enough her cheeks hurt. She wrote a couple of quick notes down in her phone then turned to him and blinked in surprise to see him studying her. He glanced at her phone, and she tucked it away. "Sorry. I'm ready to go over your plans. What did you want to discuss?"

Bryce turned around and started walking through the large room across the wood floor to the back doors. "I wanted you to take some notes on these next projects I'm planning so you can get the word out about them."

He began rambling off the different things he wanted to see done, and Carrie pulled out her phone again, turning on the recording app as she followed him. As he went on about what he wanted to see happen, she brainstormed ideas on how to get it done.

Carrie let Bryce's words wash over her as she visualized what she'd like to see done here. For the most part, he had great ideas, and with a little tweaking from her as well as a bit of training him on how to keep from scaring people away with his demanding personality, she knew he'd do great things.

Chapter Nine

Bryce stood in the back of his gallery, watching the artist talk with customers as they viewed his paintings. He couldn't believe the way the night had started so well. Carrie was a natural. She charmed everyone that came in the door and made sure they knew where they were going and what they were doing. Bryce couldn't keep his eyes off her.

Her dress shimmered in the light, and each time she moved near a display, the lighting there, intended to showcase the artwork, highlighted something new about her for him to study.

She'd done an amazing job getting this event publicized in the two weeks they'd worked on it. He had intended to keep it a small event, but when she'd explained her ideas and what it would take to jumpstart it like this, he had given her full control and told her he wanted a couple of updates as the event neared.

He hadn't seen her in person since they'd met at the outreach building where she'd shared the ideas about involving the youth in the program to spruce up the surrounding area. In that time, she'd informed him she'd contacted the businesses and city to get permission for the youth to do a clean-up and paint their buildings. He'd been so busy with his other ventures —even needing to fly to Vegas for a conference — that he still hadn't seen the building. Carrie had asked him to hold off a few more days until it was completed, but he had instructed his driver to go past the community outreach building before stopping here. Though it had been dark, he'd known a lot of painting had gone on.

He couldn't wait to see it in the daylight. But, for now he would occupy his eyes with her. Bryce watched her speak with the mayor and then one of the parents of a youth he'd seen at another event. She then smoothly transitioned to one of the wealthier couples, who were at the gallery to actually purchase some of the artwork by the up-and-coming artist.

She turned to him and smiled, then her lips moved to a slight frown, and she glanced away, returning her attention to the people around her. She glanced back at him again, and he watched her, hoping to have an idea about what she was thinking. *Why is she frowning now? Is she uncomfortable?*

The more he stared at her, the more she seemed worried, until he finally realized she was probably upset about him staring her down. She must have thought he was judging her. He was her employer, after all, and if he wasn't happy with how she did the work here, she might worry about her job.

Bryce turned his back to her, hoping to give her peace and let her know he wasn't micromanaging. He wanted her to feel comfortable and enjoy what she did.

He was sure they would sell more art tonight than at any other events he'd hosted. The way she led the guests through the gallery and stopped to discuss each work of art, introducing them to the artist, would build up a feeling of interest from the buyers that would lead to them spending money.

Bryce moved to a painting against the back wall. Very few people had stopped in front of this one, but to him, it had something special. He loved the way the darks fought against the lights, as if they had a chance, but as the flow of the image continued, the brightness overcame the dark until nothing but beauty remained. He'd never considered that a black-and-white painting could convey such emotion.

As he studied the image, contemplating his own dark thoughts, he was surprised to feel a bright presence next to him. From the smell of her perfume, he was sure it was Carrie before he caught her from the corner of his eye.

"Mr. Thomson."

"Yes?"

"Do you intend to hide from all your guests?"

Bryce turned to face her. "I'm not hiding. I'm right out here in view of anyone who wishes to speak to me."

Carrie glanced at him, but then returned her gaze to studying the artwork he'd been examining so deeply before. She shook her head softly. "You don't have to physically be somewhere else to hide. It's also about how you act and the expression on your face." She glanced at him again but didn't keep her eyes on him long. "See, even now, you are giving me a look that makes me uncomfortable, and I work for you. I'm supposed to be able to have access to you, to share updates and information. But instead, I would much rather speak to anyone else than approach you."

Bryce blinked. "My observation of the event is making you uncomfortable?" Sure he'd been watching her as an employer, but he hadn't leered at her, hadn't ogled her like other men had done tonight. He'd seen it from more than half of the men at the event, who couldn't keep their eyes off her. But maybe she was more used to being looked at that way, as a desirable woman and not as an employee. He would have to be careful in how he interacted with her because he didn't want to turn into one of the admiring idiots that saw her only for her beauty. She had much more to her than was obvious on the surface.

But since she didn't like the way he looked at her, Bryce resolved to do his best to not look her in the eye. He could focus on her eyebrow.

"You're making people uncomfortable because you don't seem to be enjoying yourself. How can you expect your guests to enjoy themselves if they feel constantly judged by you? You've made a lot of strides by getting the youth program going, and people are curious about you. But there were many people who came toward you with the intent to talk. I watched them as they neared you and then turned away. You repel them by your body language."

Bryce tilted his head back and squared his shoulders, feeling like he was being attacked for being the person he was.

"See, right there, your body language is showing me how unhappy and uncomfortable you are in my presence. That you would rather not be talking to me."

"That is not true," Bryce said. He was uncomfortable, but he wanted to talk to her. Just her though. The rest of the people attending the event meant nothing to him. He figured most of them were either overly curious about him or wanted to see what they could get from him.

"Then show it. Come talk to a few of your guests. I can't do all of the schmoozing on my own." She rested her hand on his forearm, and gave him a nudge from the side so he could make the first step and look as if he were leading her back to the group of people.

"I'm not any good at this. That's why I hired you."

"And that's why I'm doing my job. Just follow my lead. Speak if you want to, but at least come listen to the conversations. Answer the questions posed to you if you can. Come interact with the people you invited. Otherwise, none of this artwork will make the least bit of difference. If you don't give people a pleasant experience, they aren't going to come back. And there are lots of people here you want to return. Often."

Bryce took a tentative step forward, and she moved with him. The feel of her body so close to his as they walked, even though she only touched his arm, sent a shiver of pleasure over him. It had been too long since he had allowed himself to get close to a woman. He needed to remember his plan to stay away from them. Carrie was his employee, and way too young for him.

As they reached the group of people she'd steered him toward, he removed his arm from her reach as smoothly as possible, hoping it wasn't as awkward as he felt. She stayed right next to him but slipped easily into conversation with one of the clients looking for some artwork, while Bryce talked to the woman's husband.

"How do you get so many talented artists to come here?" the man asked.

Bryce glanced at Carrie as he formulated an answer, but she must not have trusted him to speak. She smiled at the man and leaned in conspiratorially. "You can't expect him to give away his secrets, Mr. Beagley."

The man chuckled. "Too true. But Charlotte is very pleased with what you've given us so far. We can't wait to see who your next artist is in a few months. She'll be sure to come back and pick her favorite from them too."

Bryce turned to Charlotte Beagley. "I am glad you've found such joy in these pieces. I have found one I'm considering adding to my personal collection as well."

Bryce could feel Carrie's eyes on him when he said that, but he didn't look at her. Charlotte peered over his shoulder, looking at some of the artwork he'd been examining before. "Really? Which one?"

Bryce blinked, feeling suddenly possessive of the black-and-white painting where Carrie had found him.

Mr. Beagley's chuckling saved him. "Oh, Charlotte, don't pester the man. You don't want to steal his favorite out from under him. Let the man keep his secrets."

Charlotte looked like she wanted to continue asking, regardless of her husband's words. Bryce felt his face turn into his mask, then immediately worried about what Carrie would say. He wondered what impression his expression had given the Beagleys. He struggled to make his face less severe, but was afraid he looked ridiculous when Carrie smiled softly as she watched him.

Carrie took action and moved closer to Charlotte Beagley. "I think I might know which one it is. Why don't we go examine a few of them and see what we can conjecture? Then I'll introduce you to the artist himself. I'm sure we can pull him away for a moment."

Charlotte grinned, and Carrie took her by the arm. Then, before Bryce could panic too much, she glanced at him, gave him a wink, and moved Charlotte toward the front of the building where the larger, more expensive pieces were. She was good, no doubt about it. He would definitely put himself in her capable hands to mold him into the type of man he needed to be in order to be successful in this crazy endeavor he'd found himself in. Why he ever thought he could continue with his grandfather's art gallery on his own, he didn't know.

As the night wore on, he comfortably spoke with more and more people, sometimes with Carrie by his side, and other times completely on his own. He knew her advice was spot on, and once he'd had a few successful interactions with a couple of clients and special guests, he felt much more capable of doing it on his own. On occasion, he wanted to go hide in the back and look at paintings on his own, but he continued to mingle, and, for the most part, he enjoyed himself. Something he hadn't expected.

When the last guest left, Carrie kicked off her shoes and sat on one of the benches positioned in front of a picture he'd seen her looking at multiple times throughout the evening. He grabbed a second glass of champagne from one of the waiters. After sitting down a foot away, he offered her the drink.

"No, thank you. I have to drive home tonight."

Bryce nodded and set her glass on the floor next to the bench. He probably shouldn't drink the one he held, but he figured he deserved it after the long night he'd just endured. He took a sip and realized he actually didn't want to down it the same way he would have if he'd done this night on his own.

"You made tonight the best one we've had at the gallery. Thank you for your assistance."

"My pleasure," Carrie said. "I enjoyed myself. And this artist is talented. He did a lot of the work selling his pieces. I'm not surprised at how well this went. Though I expected this one to sell, I'm kind of glad it didn't. I can look at it a little while longer."

She looked back at the painting in front of her, and Bryce studied it a moment as well. The artist had a knack for painting abstract shapes and colors in a way that gave feeling to the piece. This one reminded him of a broken rainbow, but instead of bringing the feeling of destruction or damage, the colors offered hope and purpose, as if the rainbow couldn't be stopped just because it was fragmented.

Broken things are still beautiful.

They sat in silence for a moment, then Carrie stretched her legs out in front of her, flexing her ankles, then sat up and arched her back, bringing his attention to the curve of her spine and the softer curves of the rest of her. His face heated, and he took another drink of his champagne before standing up.

"I'll make sure everything is locked up. You're free to go home. Thanks again for your help." He turned on his heels and took a step away from her, only to kick the other champagne glass with his foot. He heard the glass break and cursed softly.

Carrie stood up quickly and assessed the damage. "I'll be right back." She ran off toward the back room in her bare feet, hiking her skirt up a little to allow her legs more movement than the calf-length skirt would have allowed.

It gave him a view of her toned legs and he felt another flash of desire.

He shook his head, angry at himself for feeling that way about her. It was probably the champagne. *I have to stay away from any alcohol while with her.* He had to stay in complete control of his thoughts and emotions. He couldn't allow himself to have feelings for her. He gathered the broken glass and placed the pieces into his unfinished flute since he wasn't going to be drinking any more tonight.

She rushed back into the room, holding a white towel from the small serving area in the back. When she neared, he held his hand out to take the towel, but she squatted next to him and began wiping up his mess. She took a tiny crouched step forward to reach more and squeaked in pain.

"Ouch."

"What happened?" Bryce asked. "Did you step on some glass?"

"I think so," Carrie said. She stood up straight, balancing on one foot as she tried to look at the other one.

Bryce stepped around the wet spot and joined her on the other side to assist her in sitting down on the bench again. "Let me see." He knelt in front of her and lifted her injured foot, angling it toward the lights still shining on the paintings.

"I can get it." Carrie leaned forward, trying to bring her foot closer but the tight skirt prevented her.

She couldn't bend her knee enough to angle it for a good look at the outside of the foot.

"Nonsense. Now hold still so I can see if there is glass inside." A small pool of blood had collected on the outside edge of her foot near her pinkie toe. It was deeper in color than the red of her pedicured toes, but he didn't think the cut would need stitches.

He tilted her foot to the side a little, and the telltale reflection showed him where the offending glass had embedded. He pinched it carefully between his fingers, using the small edges of his nails to get a hold and pull it out.

As the glass came free, the wound started bleeding more freely, and Bryce shoved his hand into his inside breast pocket to pull out a clean handkerchief. Pressing the cloth to her foot with one hand and holding her heel with the other, he looked up at her, following the smooth leg up until his gaze finally reached her eyes. The returning look she gave him concerned him. *I shouldn't have touched her. She must think I'm a creep after ogling her like that.*

He let go of her heel but kept the cloth pressed against the foot. "If you can reach this and hold it there, I'll go find a first-aid kit."

Carrie nodded and bent forward enough to reach the handkerchief. As her hand covered his in an attempt to get a hold of the makeshift bandage, he recognized the gentle touch of a woman who was perhaps interested in more than just first aid. He pulled his hand out from under hers and rushed away.

***

Carrie watched in disappointment as Bryce ran off. She didn't understand why he was so panicked and skittish all of a sudden, but given the look she'd received from him moments ago, she knew he was just as red-blooded as any other man. But he was her boss, and she shouldn't be interested in him anyway.

As she contemplated what she should do next, one of the waiters from the evening came out with a dustpan, a bucket of water, and more towels. Bryce soon followed with a white box, and as he watched the waiter clean up the mess, he seemed to relax. Carrie felt disappointed that they wouldn't be able to talk about what had happened. She wanted to clear up any misunderstandings right away, but it wouldn't be right to discuss something like this in front of anyone.

Bryce quietly knelt in front of her again, not looking at her face as he took hold of her foot. He pulled the handkerchief off then wiped the wound clean with a small disinfectant swab before putting a bandage on it. She watched him as he gently cared for her, and her heart felt fuller than she'd expected. *He's a good man.*

"Thank you," Carrie said when he finished. She glanced at the waiter who'd almost finished wiping up the spilled champagne and knew she wouldn't be able to speak with Bryce alone as he stood and closed the first-aid kit.

"I'm sorry you were hurt. Would you like me to call you a cab?"

Carrie shook her head. "No, it doesn't hurt. I'm sure it won't interfere with driving."

Bryce nodded. "Good. I'll see you next week then. Thanks again for all your hard work on this." He turned around and left her sitting on the bench, watching his retreating back. She sighed and lifted her legs so she could turn around on the backless bench and get her shoes without walking and risk finding another piece of glass.

As she slipped on the heels, the pressure stung the cut for a moment, but she knew she'd be able to handle it long enough to get to her car. Then she'd kick them off to drive home.

She looked up at the rainbow-like painting she'd admired over the course of the evening. The price was out of her range, and she knew she couldn't afford it, or even have room to hang it in her small apartment, but she really liked the picture. It was probably a good thing this artist would be moving on, and another would be showcased soon. She didn't want to be reminded of what she had longed for from Bryce on this bench. The idea of crushing on her boss was out of the question.

Chapter Ten

Monday morning found her in Mr. Carlson's office with a few other employees, including Madison who had trained her, going over the current proposals. Carrie was relieved Mr. Carlson hadn't asked about the gala or her work with Mr. Thomson. So far, she'd been able to keep up with both jobs without much stress. The weekend had been a nice break since most of her work for the rec center transformation was done. They were on schedule for the event where the youth would display their work.

When she'd told the owners she would cover the cost of the paint and labor for their permission to decorate, they'd been a little hesitant. But after showing them the designs from the artists they could pick from, they'd warmed up to the idea. After that, it had been easy getting the youth together to put it all into motion. The walls inside the rec center were almost completed. The murals were taking shape nicely, and she couldn't wait to see the finished project. Eric hadn't stopped talking about it since he'd begun working on them.

She tried to put Bryce's projects out of her mind and focus on the ad agency instead. It took a little work, but she managed to only think of Bryce and the art exhibit last Friday night twenty times or so. The small cut on her foot was healed enough she didn't need a bandage anymore, but she could remember the feel of his caress on her skin as he'd cared for her wound.

She slipped her heels off under the desk for a moment and wiggled her toes, then slipped her feet back into the shoes. Madison and Mr. Carlson were discussing the newest clients and the plans for commercials they had in the works. Carrie took notes, as usual, so she'd know which clients to contact and update. When the meeting wrapped up, Carrie gathered her things, and Madison waited for her at the door.

"I heard you've been helping in a youth outreach program."

"Yes." Carrie glanced at Madison. "Mr. Carlson donated some hours to the project, and I was happy to get involved. I think it will be extra helpful to kids like Eric."

Madison nodded. "I think it sounds like a great idea. I've never heard of Bryce Thomson, though. Is he from the area?"

Carrie hesitated a moment, not sure how much of what she knew about Bryce she should share. "He's from Idaho, but his grandfather lived here. Bryce took over his business."

"Oh, was his grandfather Matthew Shields?"

"Yeah, did you know Mr. Shields?" Carrie asked.

"Not personally, but my sister did," Madison said. "He started the art gallery, right?"

"I believe so." Trying to change the subject away from Bryce, Carrie said, "Did you enjoy your honeymoon in Hawaii?"

Madison's face lit up. "Oh my goodness, it was wonderful. Part of me wishes I could have taken Milo along with us, but I'm so glad just Stephen and I went. The Hawaiian Islands are the perfect place for a honeymoon."

Carrie grinned. "Yeah, I'm sure Milo was fine without his parents. I'm so glad you had a good time. I want to take a trip there some day."

"You should," Madison agreed. "My favorite was the Big Island. Less crowded and still had such beautiful things to go see. We'll take another trip out there with Milo, next time in February. Milo wants to see the whales. Stephen says that's one of the best times."

They chatted for a few minutes before Madison checked her watch. "Sorry, I've got to run get ready for my clients soon. Did you need any help with these accounts before I go?"

"No, I've got it. Thanks, though."

Carrie moved into her office and organized the notes according to what was most important. The buzz of her phone alerted her to a text.

Bryce: The program director said one of our volunteer mentors is unable to make it for tonight.

Carrie: Which one?

Bryce: He'll get in touch with you. See if you can find someone. Thanks.

Carrie looked at the phone, trying to figure out what Bryce had meant. Before she could send another question to him, her phone rang. "Hello?"

"Ms. Winters? This is Anthony Houston. Mr. Thomson said you might have an idea on where we could find someone who would fill in for one of the classes. The guy doing digital design isn't able to make it anymore. Said something about a family emergency. And the kids need someone to take over that class. We've got more than a dozen students doing that one."

"Digital design? Like photo manipulation and such?"

"Yeah, pretty much. Do you know anyone?"

"I took a few classes in college. I could cover for a bit. Do you think the guy will be back? How long do we need a replacement?"

Anthony didn't answer for a moment. "Not sure. The message I got wasn't really detailed. Would it be a problem if it was for a long time?"

"I'm not sure how much I can actually commit to, but for tonight, I could fill in."

"Wonderful. Thank you, Ms. Winters," Anthony said. "I'll text you the details." He hung up before Carrie could say anything more.

She stared at the phone, wondering what she'd just gotten herself into. She hadn't done photo manipulation on her own for a while, since most of her time at the agency was involved in more of the business and accounts aspect, but she did have the image manipulation program on her computer. It should be easy enough to look over and remind herself what she'd need to do.

Text after text buzzed on her phone from Anthony, and she took a slow breath. These kids had already done an intro to basics so she wouldn't be able to start from scratch. She scanned the messages and decided she would just go there and chat with the kids, find out what they knew, how much the other guy had taught them, and where they wanted to go from there. Maybe show them some of the things magazines and advertisements could do with digital manipulation.

She knew Bryce had purchased some computers for the program, and they had the photo-manipulating software on them. She'd have time to pick up a quick bite from Jesse's Grill before heading over to the rec center. She needed to let Eric know her plans.

Carrie: I'll be helping in one of the classes tonight. I can get you guys started, but can you make sure the murals are worked on?

Eric: Sure. We're really close. Probably finish tonight.

Carrie: Awesome.

***

When Bryce arrived at the rec center to meet with the director of the building, he was stunned by the transformations that had taken place. The trash cans had been painted, different whimsical scenes on each one. The sidewalks had temporary paint on them, depicting holiday themes from Thanksgiving to Christmas. A few had been done as murals on the sides of businesses, but the one that surprised him the most was on his own building. The painting seamlessly moved from a starry night interspersed with spring flowers to a summer beach scene that blended into fall colors and snowy landscapes. It was amazing.

He moved closer to the group surrounding Carrie and listened in to the conversations. He smiled when he heard her directing praise to the youth who had done the artwork. Originally, he had mostly wanted to give the kids in the city a place to go where they wouldn't get into mischief, but Carrie had taken it further than that. She'd helped them take pride in their surroundings, and he knew the neighborhood would benefit from these kids having a sense of community.

Bryce couldn't help but feel proud of what they'd accomplished. He checked in on the other classrooms to see how many kids they had using the facility. Each classroom and art studio or sculpting room had a handful at least. Given that the program had opened less than a month ago, he knew interest would grow as the word got out.

I should find someone to teach dance or theater. Spring should be soon enough. He didn't want to stretch things too thin. And though Carrie was highly capable of a lot, he knew if he gave her too much all at once, he'd risk burning her out.

He returned to the artists working on the mural but couldn't find Carrie anywhere among them. He moved closer to see if she was among the group near the wall with the paints and brushes.

"Hey, Mr. T," Eric, Carrie's brother said. Bryce wondered what had possessed the kid to call him that.

It wasn't as if Thomson was a hard name to say, but at least he wasn't calling him by his first name. Not that he would have corrected the kid, but he preferred to not be on too familiar terms.

"Hello, Eric. Have you seen Ms. Winters?"

"Carrie's teaching a class."

"She's teaching one?"

"Yeah, the digital design one, I think. Said the guy couldn't make it, and she's covering for a bit."

Bryce turned away from the group of painters and took a few steps toward the classroom with the computers. He stopped short and turned around. "You all have done a fantastic job on these murals. I'm impressed."

Eric nodded. "Thanks. It's been so cool to do this. No one has ever let me just do my thing on this kind of scale before. We're having a blast."

The other kids voiced their agreement, and Bryce chatted with them for a moment, feeling their excitement as they told him of the process it took to make the mural. When he finally pulled himself away from the group, he moved over to the classroom where Carrie would likely be.

He peeked through the open door and watched as she chatted and interacted with the teens. She wasn't much older than they were. She looked a little more mature, but the way she easily talked with them and related to each on a personal level reinforced his impression that he was too old for her. He'd been relieved to get away from the kids talking about the mural, and here Carrie seemed to be thriving in the attention these kids gave her. She was much closer in age to them than to him.

Bryce stepped away from the door before she noticed and headed to find Anthony. He needed to know why he'd picked Carrie to cover for the class. He didn't want her to do too much. Because he had a few ideas he wanted to run by her, the fact she wasn't available to him was irritating.

***

Bryce had avoided meeting with her in person for days. Tonight would be the first time he would see her since the night he'd watched her teaching the design class. He'd been in contact through texts and emails, but when she'd called to speak to him in person, he'd let it go to voicemail then texted his answer. He didn't want to hear her voice. She was too tempting, but tonight he would have to talk to her. And he would stay far away from the champagne. He needed every last bit of wits with him as he spent time with her.

He knew Carrie had arrived more than an hour earlier and had been visiting with the artist of the month. Krissy Kandor was a talented photographer whose work had become more and more popular. The pieces she had on display tonight were breathtaking and would be sure to bring in crowds of buyers. He wouldn't be surprised to see Charlotte Beagley again tonight.

Bryce hoped he wouldn't have to talk to Charlotte long.

One of the staff at the gallery approached him, and he turned to answer questions about the placement of some of the smaller prints the artist had provided. When he'd satisfied all the questions, he turned to check on something else and bumped into Carrie, who'd joined him, nearly knocking her down in the process. His hands went out instinctively, and he steadied her.

"Ms. Winters," he said. "I'm sorry. I didn't see you there."

She shook her head as if to dismiss it, and he reluctantly pulled his hands away from her upper arms where he still held on.

"How can I help you?" Bryce asked.

Carrie smiled. "I was going to ask the same thing. We've got less than thirty minutes before the guests will start arriving. I've made sure Krissy is prepped and ready to go. Is there anything else you'd like me to do? We haven't had a chance to actually touch base for a while."

Bryce nodded slowly. "I believe we're ready. The catering staff is set up with the hors d'oeuvres and drinks, and we've got everything set up to take sales. You can relax for a few minutes. I don't imagine you've had much down time lately since taking on the digital design class."

"It doesn't take much. The kids are well-versed in the program. They mostly just need the time and the equipment and can do it all on their own with little help from me. I'm basically there as a sounding board or opinion giver."

"I appreciate you stepping in to do that, but when I contacted you about finding someone, I didn't mean to imply you needed to teach."

"I didn't take it as that. Though when Anthony found out I knew about digital design, he quickly encouraged me to fill in for that night. I planned to just give it long enough for us to find a more permanent replacement, but I'm enjoying it. Your original instructor will be back in a few weeks. I can help that long."

Bryce nodded. "With the project reveals planned for these youth artists in mid-January, do you think we'll have enough to display?"

"Absolutely. From what I've heard from all the other artist mentors, each kid has at least one project. As I see it, you've got a couple options. You can have each teen pick their best piece and bring it to the gallery here for a night kind of like tonight. Or you could use the different artistic mediums, digital art displayed the same week your mentor does their work. Then follow weekly with a new style… oil paints, acrylics, watercolors, photography, sculptures and so on. That would tie up your gallery though. So, if you were to have each of the students display all their work at the rec center, you could make it a little less formal and get the family members and friends of the participants to come. That would spread the word better, and you'd get more youth participating."

"Each idea has merit. Which do you recommend?" Bryce asked.

"I'd suggest starting off in the rec center. And, as the project grows, you can begin inviting the youth to submit one work to be displayed at your gallery. Many would love to have a chance to sell their work, but they might not understand the whole commission thing. There is also the option of finding local businesses and city buildings to host the artwork for a while… schools, libraries, city office buildings, and so on. That could be where you hold the different mediums displayed for a month or two at a time."

Bryce nodded. "I like where you're going with this. We'll have to think on it and make a few more plans. Write up an outline of the different options, and we'll go from there."

Carrie wrote something in her phone. "Anything else?"

"Not right now." He glanced around the room, hoping for something to do to get himself away from the woman before he did something stupid and asked her to dinner where they could go over the plans. When he caught sight of their guest artist, he knew that was his out. "Excuse me. I think I should take your advice and go speak with Ms. Kandor, make sure I know enough about her work to speak to the guests tonight."

Carrie grinned and placed her hand on his arm. "Yay, we're finally making progress." She looked him over, and, before he knew what was happening, she was straightening his tie. Her hands smoothed down the lapels of his suit then trailed down his chest a few inches before she pulled her hands back.

From the way she acted, it didn't seem to mean anything, but the spike in his heart rate betrayed him once again. He was very much not immune to her, and the more he found himself in her presence, the more he wished he could actually be with her. She walked away, and his gaze followed her for much longer than it should have.

He was in trouble. For a moment, he considered firing her so he wouldn't have to be in the same room anymore, but that was a stupider idea than hiring her in the first place had been.

No, I've put myself in a mess, yet I'm not sure I want out right away. Confusion about anything was a foreign emotion. Too bad he'd sworn off drinking tonight. He could use a little alcohol to calm his nerves.

Chapter Eleven

"Eric, are you ready to go?"

"Almost." His voice from the back room down the hallway echoed through the empty apartment. Abby had gone to her grandparents for Thanksgiving, and Carrie's mom was traveling with her new husband. Eric hadn't wanted to go to Shane's, who had probably only invited him out of obligation, so they had decided to do a small feast together. But before that, they'd go volunteer at the soup kitchen.

"Can I drive?" Eric asked as he came out of his room and pulled a knitted beanie over his dark hair.

"Sure. Where's your car parked?"

Eric rolled his eyes.

"Oh, that's right," Carrie said. "You don't have one."

"Come on, Carrie. I won't wreck it."

Carrie held up her arm, still in the cast for another week. "Yeah, I thought the same thing. It happens. And I'm not interested in having to go through the whole mess with insurance and crap."

Eric frowned but didn't argue the point. He pulled on his hoodie then went to the front door and headed to the car. She locked the door behind her and joined him in the parking lot of the small apartment complex. She debated for a moment about whether she should let him drive. He was seventeen and a good kid when he wasn't getting in trouble for ditching school. But since becoming involved in Bryce's outreach program, he'd really made some strides.

"Hey." She tossed him the keys over the top of the car and, as he caught them, the excitement in his eyes made her smile. "If you scratch my car even the tiniest bit, I'll never let you drive it again." Her threat wasn't all that powerful, but Eric nodded.

"I'll treat her better than my girlfriend."

"You don't have a girlfriend."

"That's what you think." Eric grinned as he walked around the car to the driver's side.

"Well, well, well… I think the way you'll pay me back for this kindness is to tell me all about her."

When Eric didn't complain, Carrie's eyes widened again. *Wow, he must really like her if he's willing to talk about her.* "How long have you been dating?"

Eric shrugged. "A while."

"As in days, weeks or months?" Carrie asked. "How did I miss this? Does she go to your school? Where'd you meet?"

Eric glanced at her as he pulled out of the parking spot. "She's not in my school, but we met at the rec center that first day. She's in Leslie's group."

Carrie tried to picture all the kids involved with Leslie. Not many of them worked on clay sculpting, but she knew of at least four girls in that class. "What's her name?"

"Kourtney."

Carrie studied Eric as he drove. "Is she the one with the long brown hair, or the one with the buzz cut on one side?"

"Buzz."

"Ah, she's cute. A sweetie too." Carrie watched Eric's face as the praise she'd given his girlfriend obviously found a place in his soul. "So have you taken her out?"

"No car."

Carrie nodded. "Sucks to be young with no job, huh?"

He gave her a quick look with narrowed eyes and she snorted.

"Well, it does. I was that way once."

"So can I borrow your car to take her out?" Eric asked.

"Um, I'm not sure about that. Maybe we could double, though."

Eric shook his head. "Um, no."

"Why not?" Carrie asked.

"Who would you go with?" Eric asked. "Far as I know, you're more single than the number one."

"I could find a date." As soon as she said it, Carrie had a crazy desire to ask Bryce out, until Eric crushed that thought.

"And no offense, Carrie, but you're kinda too old to have fun with high school juniors."

Carrie cocked her head to the side. "Yeah, and I'm for certain too old to let my little brother drive my car again." She shook her head. "Don't think my senior citizen automobile discounts would cover a teen driver not on my insurance. Better pull over, sonny, so I can take over the driving."

"I didn't mean it like that, Carrie. I just mean, the types of stuff we'd be interested in doing wouldn't be something you'd want to do. You're more cultured than that. Hanging out at the movies or going to play video games in someone's basement isn't your thing."

"And what exactly is my thing?" Carrie asked. She was only twenty-four. And though she hadn't gone dancing for a while, she still enjoyed hitting the night clubs.

"You're more into culture and stuff. Like those galas you keep attending."

"You do know I work for Mr. Thomson. I'm paid to go to those."

"Really?" Eric asked. "I thought you went 'cause you liked spending time with Mr. T."

Carrie whipped her head around to look at Eric. "What?"

"I thought you just went to hang out around him. He's more your age, and the two of you seem pretty friendly. I figured you two had a thing for each other."

Carrie's mouth dropped open. Sure, she thought Bryce was a great guy and very nice to look at, but she had never flirted with him or done anything to indicate she liked him. *Have I?*

"I do not have a thing for Bryce."

"Sure you don't." Eric glanced at her then back at the road when she pointed out the front window. "Be serious, Carrie. I'll bet if he wasn't your boss, you'd be all over him."

"I would not." Carrie crossed her arms over her chest.

"Whatever."

"Just shut up and drive. We're almost there."

Eric bit his bottom lip as if he were trying to keep from smiling. *Is he high? I hope no one else thinks I have the hots for my boss.* She racked her brain, trying to remember all the interactions she'd had with him, in public and in private. She'd treated him like every other man she worked with, apart from that night she'd cut her foot, but no one would have seen that interaction besides the waiter, and she was sure she'd been on her best behavior while he was around.

Of course, with her trying to teach him how to be social and to interact with his clients and the artists more, maybe she had been a little too intimate and friendly. And what had Bryce thought of her? Given the way he'd been ignoring her lately, he must have felt uncomfortable with her behavior.

Eric pulled into the soup kitchen lot. He put the car in park and pulled out the keys, then handed them to Carrie without a word.

"Thanks," she said.

Eric pointed at the two possible entrances. "Should we go to the front doors or over by where the delivery trucks drop stuff off?"

"Don't know. Do you see anyone?"

"Someone came out the front doors as I turned into the parking lot," Eric said.

"So let's try that." Carrie climbed out of the car and pushed the lock button on her keys as soon as Eric got out of the driver's side. She tucked the keys in her pocket and walked around the car to join him as they headed toward the building.

Eric pointed to a dark car in the far corner of the lot. "Is that Mr. T?"

Carrie stopped walking and stared at where Eric pointed. "I don't know."

"I think that's his car — or one just like his. I checked it out that night at the first event at the rec center." Eric squinted a little in the mid-morning light. "Yeah, I'm pretty sure it's his."

"What makes you sure?" Carrie asked.

Eric grinned. "'Cause that's him carrying a box of potatoes from the truck over there." He pointed in the opposite direction at a couple of white vans and trucks with a half-dozen people carrying boxes into the building. "Guess we could join them."

Carrie nodded numbly, not sure she wanted to be in the same place with Bryce Thomson right now, especially when she didn't know how to act around him. *Why is he here? He had to drive clear across town to help at this soup kitchen.* Carrie shook her head. It didn't matter how far away it was. He was the type of guy who would help wherever he thought it was needed. One more thing to add to what she admired in him.

Now if only she knew the best way to proceed. She couldn't ignore him completely, but after hearing what Eric thought of her interactions with Bryce, she didn't want to do the same thing she'd always done.

Hopefully, they wouldn't need to interact much today anyway. She would find out where they needed help and get to it.

She moved into line behind Eric and glanced behind her when she felt someone approach. It wasn't

Bryce, and for that she was thankful. She wasn't ready to talk to him. The guy in the truck handed Eric a box of potatoes then gave Carrie two huge cans of sweet corn. She tucked one under each arm, her cast giving her a little trouble, but she adjusted the can and followed Eric into the building.

As soon as she spotted someone who looked to be in charge, she carried the corn over to the counter then moved to speak with the man. "Can I get started on potatoes or something, or would it be more helpful to keep bringing things in?"

"Peeling the taters would be awesome." He scurried over to a box on the counter and rummaged through it, looking for something. "I've got some peelers here. Have at it. Once you've got them done, you can slice 'em up to get them boiling."

Carrie got right to work and had a fourth of a twenty-pound box peeled when she heard someone pull up a chair and sit next to her.

Bryce's smooth voice spoke, sending shivers down her spine. "May I join you?"

She nodded, not wanting to speak, and reached for another potato.

"I saw Eric out there helping set up tables. He wasn't sure where you'd gone."

Carrie glanced at him then returned her attention to peeling. "He saw me last time he brought in some things."

Bryce didn't speak for a moment as he got his peeler and potatoes started. He'd moved close and shared the same bucket she used to catch the peels. She caught a whiff of his cologne. His clothes were much more muted and different than how she was used to seeing him. A polo shirt with the top couple buttons undone made him look more relaxed and friendly than his suits or blazers.

But the casual clothes didn't diminish his sex appeal in the slightest. In fact, she thought he looked hotter than ever, and a lot younger. They worked in silence for a few minutes, the only sounds coming from the smooth slicing of the peelers and the potato skins dropping into the bucket. The door to the kitchen opened, and a few other volunteers entered the room, bringing with them a breeze that stirred the air enough to send another whiff of his intoxicating scent.

"What kind of cologne do you wear?" she asked, then wished she hadn't. *What kind of question is that? He's going to think I want him.* She tried to think of some way to cover for her outburst. "I still need to do a little Christmas shopping and thought maybe Eric might like that. He's got a new girlfriend, and all…" Carrie trailed off at the look Bryce gave her. "Never mind. He probably would want to pick his own out." She tossed the finished potato into the bowl with the others, then, deciding it was getting pretty full, she put the peeler down and reached for the bowl. "I'll go wash these up and get them ready for slicing. You can keep going."

She took a slow breath as she walked away from Bryce, giving herself a stern talking to. She didn't need to go all freaky on him now that she'd realized she actually had feelings for the man.

***

Bryce wasn't sure what had changed, but Carrie didn't seem too interested in speaking with him. Of course, as they prepared and served the food at the soup kitchen for the people coming for Thanksgiving dinner, there wasn't a lot of time to interact.

He'd helped with the potatoes, but she'd been short with him, and not very talkative. After they finished the peeling, Carrie had insisted that she could do all the chopping on her own, so Bryce helped Eric set up tables. He'd had more luck talking to him than he had with Carrie, which was odd, since Eric was a lot more timid than his social sister. Eric told him about the mural project.

Bryce hadn't known Carrie had been the one to suggest the theme for it, but he thought the way all the seasons tied together had been an excellent choice. Everything she did seemed to fall into place just right. He was lucky to have found her. He decided to stay away from her for the rest of the morning as the meal was prepared so he didn't scare her off. He kept busy enough with his assignments, but she was never too far away he couldn't observe her on occasion.

When the guests started arriving for their meals, she was at one end of the table dishing up potatoes while he made sure the kitchen supplied the table with refills. When he brought her a pot of potatoes, she smiled and thanked him, just as she had the others who'd brought her refills before, but something about the way she spoke made him feel special. Maybe he'd misread her behavior before.

He knew social cues weren't his strength, but her smiles sure did warm his heart.

The meal was almost over, and most of the food had been consumed. He noticed there were a few people who hadn't received some of the extra side dishes, but thankfully there had been enough turkey and potatoes. And next year, he'd make sure there were more. They'd also run out of pumpkin pie, but there was enough apple pie and ice cream to serve those still coming through.

As the last diner left, the volunteers began the job of cleaning up. With many helpers, it wouldn't take too long. At least he hoped it would be quick. He was tired and ready to go home, but as the realization hit that he'd be all alone, he no longer felt as eager to leave.

Bryce watched as Eric pulled out his phone. He looked excited then glanced over at Carrie and frowned a moment before looking back at the phone. He moved over to his sister. Bryce couldn't hear what they were saying, but he could tell Carrie wasn't very happy about whatever Eric had told her.

Curiosity got the better of him, and Bryce moved closer to the table where they were standing and pulled the paper table covering off.

Carrie shook her head but didn't look too disappointed. "Can't believe you'll abandon me on Thanksgiving to go to your girlfriend's house."

Eric shifted his weight from one foot to the other. "I'll be back for dinner. I just won't be there to help you make it, but you never let me in the kitchen anyway, so what does it matter if I'm at home or at Kourtney's?"

She sighed and pulled out her keys then passed them over to Eric who whooped then got busy sending a message on his phone, probably to the girlfriend.

Bryce spoke. "I can drive you home if you'd like."

Carrie startled, apparently not realizing he was right there. She put her hand over her heart and shook her head. "Thanks, but I can get a cab. I'm sure you've got other things going on with your life. Don't you have someone you're going to spend Thanksgiving with?"

Bryce shook his head. "I'm flying solo for the holiday. My parents and grandparents have all passed."

Carrie looked at Bryce. "Are you planning on having a Thanksgiving dinner?"

"I ate turkey here."

Carrie smiled softly. "It was an okay turkey, but I've got a small one I'll be cooking tonight. It'll only take a couple of hours to get a full-on Thanksgiving meal ready. Are you open enough this afternoon that we could go over some of your plans for the next few months while the turkey is cooking?" She pulled out her phone and looked at her calendar. "We've got two events before New Year's and the kickoff exhibit mid-January. Doing a little planning right away would help me get a head start on things so I can be the most productive with my available time."

Bryce studied her for a moment. "I am open. This was the only thing I had planned for the day so far. And a real turkey dinner sounds better than the Chinese takeout I was going to get."

Carrie tucked her phone away. "Eric and I even made pies last night, but we kinda went overboard and have way too many for just the two of us to eat. We'll definitely need some help."

"I am an excellent pie eater. I would be happy to help you with that."

"Then I will accept a ride home, but I'm going to make you peel potatoes again."

Bryce nodded. "I'm not afraid." He examined his fingers for a moment. "It's been a long time since I cut myself with a peeler."

Carrie grabbed her jacket and headed toward the door. "Let's go then."

As they left the building, Bryce kept pace with her then rushed forward to open the door before she reached it. She let him, and as they walked to his car, he opened the passenger door and assisted her in getting in then walked around to the driver side and slid into the car.

"Would you like to tell me the address or put it into the navigation system?"

"The navigation systems always get it wrong. It'll be easier if I direct you," Carrie said.

***

Carrie told him which streets to take, and, between the directions, they chatted easily about the meal they'd helped serve. They said nothing about the few uncomfortable minutes they'd shared as they peeled potatoes, and Carrie wondered if she should bring it up to apologize for being so short with him.

It wasn't like her to be so moody, but after her discussion with Eric on the way there, she had been out of sorts. She'd felt a little awkward at first with him so close in the kitchen, but throughout the day, he'd been completely professional. Since they would be discussing work over Thanksgiving dinner, she knew things would remain professional. She didn't have to worry about anything.

Carrie hoped her apartment was still okay. She mentally went through each room, trying to remember if everything had been put away. Eric's room would have been closed. And Abby's room was always clean. She couldn't function without everything in its proper place. She wasn't quite feng shui strict, but close. The kitchen had the pies on the counter under some towels, and they'd cleaned up the mess last night thankfully.

She shouldn't have to worry about what he thought. It wasn't as if she'd brought him home on a date. It was a business meeting, just at her house. He wasn't in his regular suit and tie — or even his blazer. This was very casual. Eric would be back in time for dinner, and they would just be eating a meal as friends. *Eric better return in time.*

Chapter Twelve

Bryce closed his eyes as he chewed the moist turkey. "I have never, in my whole life, had a turkey this soft and juicy before."

"Isn't it the best?" Carrie said. "I had a boyfriend in college who taught me the trick of using a can of pineapple inside the bird."

"Your boyfriend cooked you a turkey?" Bryce asked, feeling a strange sensation. *I'm not jealous.* He didn't have feelings for Carrie. At least not romantic ones, and besides, she wasn't still seeing the guy, so why did he have that flash of annoyance at the casual way she'd said boyfriend?

"Yeah, he also made the most amazing pies."

"Did he teach you how to do those pies as well?" Bryce asked, glancing at the pies on the counter waiting for their turn at the table.

"I already knew how to do pies. My grandma taught me before she passed away. But he did give me a couple of tips on how to make the crust flakier, so it's kind of a blending of recipes."

Bryce nodded. "If they are anywhere as good as this turkey, I can't wait to try."

"Oh, I can promise they're good. In fact, if you hadn't come over, I might have skipped the turkey till tomorrow and just eaten pie tonight." She leaned in a little closer. "Don't tell anyone, but I've eaten an entire pie on my own in one day."

Bryce smiled at her playful attitude. "Really?"

"Yup. Breakfast, lunch, and dinner."

"Sounds completely reasonable to me," Bryce said. "The fruit alone makes it healthy."

"Exactly." Carrie grinned, making Bryce's heart skip a beat. "And I made sure to have some whipped cream too. So the dairy was covered."

"An excellent choice to pair with it." He looked at the pies again. "I'm thinking most pies benefit from the smoothness of the cream. But I must ask, is whipped cream a better choice than ice cream?" He put his fork down and rubbed his chin. "In my opinion, nothing can compare to a rich French vanilla."

Carrie put her fork down too and leaned back against her chair as if considering his claim. "I suppose ice cream does have its merits, but if you aren't careful in picking the right brand, the French vanilla can overpower the fruit. Though the raspberry is tart enough, the ice cream would be a better choice than just the plain whipping cream."

Bryce nodded slowly. "It does require a bit of forethought to get the perfect pairing. I am pleased you take your desserts seriously enough to study the best options."

Carrie picked up her fork again and took a bite of her mashed potatoes. She'd let him make them, and he was happy they'd turned out so well. And the gravy she'd whipped up using the partially sweet turkey drippings had his mouth watering for another bite.

They chatted happily and enjoyed the rest of the meal, and Bryce couldn't help being glad Eric hadn't returned yet. He'd texted Carrie an hour ago to let her know he'd be a little later and to start without him. When it was time to pull out the pie, Bryce had very little room left, but he would try each one of the pies, if it killed him.

Carrie opened her freezer. "Uh, bad news."

Bryce turned from the sink where he'd placed the dirty dishes. "What?"

"I don't have any ice cream."

Bryce joined her to look in the freezer. "What kind of woman are you?" he asked with mock surprise. "Don't all girls your age have cartons of it as a stockpile against bad dates?"

Carrie raised an eyebrow at him. "Where did you get that goofy idea?"

Bryce felt her warmth as an obvious difference from the coolness seeping out of the freezer. He lost his train of thought for a moment as he contemplated how nice it would feel to snuggle up to that warmth. As she closed the freezer door, he came back to his senses. "You don't do ice cream binges every time a date goes wrong?"

Carrie rolled her eyes. "Well, first off, I don't have a lot of dates going wrong. I don't have a lot of time to date anyway. And another thing, with Eric living with us, any ice-cream Abby and I might have is often stolen late at night by a hungry teenage boy." She took a small step to the side and opened the fridge door, making Bryce step back a little. "Besides, if I ate ice-cream every night, it would be a little harder to keep my girlish figure."

Bryce's gaze trailed down said figure, and he once again had to remind himself she was an employee, and he couldn't afford to have any thoughts of that kind about her.

"Guess we'll have to make do with the whipping cream."

Bryce looked over her shoulder inside the refrigerator for the familiar canister that would dispense the whipped topping but didn't see anything like that. Instead, Carrie pulled out a small cardboard carton that looked like a small box of milk. Carrie gathered a couple of things including a small hand mixer. "If you'll cut the pies, I'll make up the whipping cream."

Bryce watched her as she maneuvered her way around the kitchen, and he realized he'd missed out on a lot with his ex-wife. Margery had never been one to cook, and though Bryce could do enough to not starve, it had been extra hard trying to do the meals as well as start up his business. They'd had freezer meals too often or had ordered takeout so much he'd wondered where their paycheck had gone. And though now he had enough money to hire a housekeeper who also cooked him meals throughout the week, there was something amazing about seeing it prepared in front of him, and he longed to have that in his life again.

Someday he'd have to find someone with skills in the kitchen. He looked at the pies. "Which one should I cut?"

Carrie glanced over her shoulder. "All of them."

Bryce grinned, happy he'd actually get to try them all. "Yes, ma'am." He had them sliced and on the table by the time she brought the bowl of topping. She held up a beater she'd used to whip the cream and offered it to him as she licked the second one. He watched her in surprise as her pink tongue cleaned off one edge of the metal before she turned it and licked the next side.

"Eric loves to lick the beater, but, since he's not here, you get the honor."

Bryce took the beater from her, brushing his fingers across her hand as he retrieved it. She was slowly killing him, and from what he could tell, she had no idea of her effect on him. She looked at him as if he were just a friend. Nothing in her expression indicated she found him interesting or attractive at all. He would do well to put her out of his mind and just enjoy her friendship. He licked the beater and grinned. "I can't believe I'm saying this, but your whipped cream might be able to hold its own in place of ice cream today."

Carrie winked at him. "Let's hope so. I added extra vanilla just for you." She slid a slice of each pie onto a clean plate then scooped up a large spoonful of her whipped topping for each piece. "The moment of truth."

Bryce picked up his fork and took a bite of the raspberry one first. He sighed with pleasure when the tartness of the berries mixed with the sweet, smooth cream. "This is amazing."

"French-vanilla amazing?" Carrie asked.

"Better."

Carrie chuckled. "I'm glad." She picked up her fork and tasted her pies, one at a time, and he couldn't take his eyes off her. She talked a little, and he watched her mouth move as she formed each word. He had to remind himself to look into her eyes instead of at her full lips. And when he struggled to keep himself from falling into the depths of her sparkling eyes, he focused instead on his pies.

When he'd reached his last two bites, the door opened, and Eric came in. A strange blend of relief and disappointment washed over him. With someone there to distract him from this woman who had put a spell on him over the course of the evening, he could make it out of there without doing something he'd regret later.

Bryce had heard it said often that a way to a man's heart was through his stomach. He'd never actually believed it before now, but he was well on his way to losing his heart to her, and he doubted she really wanted it.

"You started the pie without me?" Eric asked.

"Of course we did," Carrie said. "You never said when you'd be getting here, and to not wait for you for dinner."

Eric grabbed a plate and fork and pulled up a chair. "For dinner, but not for the pie. No one makes pies as good as yours." He took a bite of one the second he got to the table without putting it on his plate first. "Kourtney's mom's pies were store-bought." Eric put one of each pie slice on his plate and scooped double helpings of the whipped cream. "Mmm." Eric looked at Bryce. "Good, aren't they?"

Bryce nodded. "Best I've had."

Carrie blushed, and Bryce smiled, happy to see his words meant something to her. He wondered if he should say anything more, but now with Eric there, he didn't want an audience for his inability to talk to a woman. He picked up their plates and took them to the sink, before rinsing them off in preparation for loading the dishwasher.

"You don't have to do those, Bryce," Carrie said.

Bryce loved the way her voice caressed his name. It wasn't the usual "*Mr. Thomson.*" She apparently felt comfortable enough to call him by his first name. "I believe it's customary, at least in my household growing up. Thanksgiving dishes were done by the men since the women did the meal."

"Now that sounds like a fabulous tradition."

"No way," Eric said around a mouthful of food.

"Man up, Eric. You can do it," Bryce said.

Eric nodded and finished his bite of pie, then joined Bryce at the sink. "We watching the movie, Carrie?"

Carrie shrugged. "I don't know. Hadn't really thought about it."

Eric took his plate to the sink. "Come on, Carrie." He tilted his head toward Bryce. "If you're making me do this tradition with him, seems only fair that he should participate in our movie ritual."

126

Bryce glanced at Carrie and saw her bite her lip as if considering, then she shrugged and smiled. "I suppose." She looked at Bryce. "What do you say to *Piranazis: The Secrets of Atlantis?*"

"I don't think I've ever seen that movie."

"Then you'll have to stay and give yourself some culture," Eric said.

Bryce looked at his watch. He didn't have anything else to do tonight, and it was only a quarter after seven. He looked at Carrie, hoping to see some indication to whether she really wanted him there. He had monopolized most of her day, and he didn't want to overstay his welcome.

When she smiled at him and nodded, Bryce felt himself cave. "Thank you. I will stay."

***

Carrie watched from the corner of her eye as Bryce endured the first five minutes of the movie Eric had insisted they watch. It had started as a joke when they were young. Their older brother, Shane, brought home some horrid B-list movie from a video rental store, saying it should have been one of the best movies of the year, and made everyone sit through it.

In order to tolerate the show, Carrie had started adding her own words as the characters forced them to submit to sub-par acting, and Eric easily picked up on it and added his own corny dialogue.

Before sitting on the loveseat he occupied, Eric had whispered in her ear that they should watch the movie as if they were serious about it being a family tradition, just to see what Bryce would do. Carrie didn't think it would be a good idea to drag it on too long. But for a while, she enjoyed watching him suffer through it.

Eric glanced at her, and she smiled. He tilted his chin toward Bryce sitting on the other end of the sofa where Carrie sat, and she glanced at Bryce again. The man rubbed his forehead as if the show were giving him a headache. Carrie chuckled, and Eric took a slow breath, obviously trying to keep from laughing. Carrie nodded to him, and Eric decreased the movie volume and began the corny dialogue they'd rehearsed so many times.

Bryce lifted his head as Carrie giggled at Eric's theatrics. She glanced at Bryce, hoping he would be a good sport about it. The kid looked up to him, and Carrie knew Eric would be devastated if Bryce said anything negative.

Bryce studied Eric for a moment and leaned back against the couch, closing his eyes. "Thank heavens."

Carried laughed aloud, and Eric chuckled a moment before continuing with his parts.

Bryce shook his head as a wide grin spread out across his face. "I was worried you two were serious about this horrid movie." He turned his head toward her but still kept reclining against the couch. "I was trying to figure out a polite way to excuse myself. Was even tempted to fake a text so I'd have to answer and leave."

"What?" Carrie asked in mock offense. "You fake meetings to get out of something you aren't happy with?" She paused for a moment. "Have you done that before?"

Bryce didn't answer but pulled out his phone. "Oh, did I just get a text?"

Carrie pushed his shoulder softly. "Shut up." She looked back at the movie. With Eric providing the new words, she was certain it would be much more enjoyable, but she couldn't blame Bryce if he wanted to leave. She knew she needed to give him an out if he needed it. "Though you are more than welcome to stay and play along, if you do have other things you need to get to, we understand."

Eric stopped his lines and interrupted. "No, Mr. T. You've got to stay and listen to Carrie's part. She does the best damsel in distress."

Carrie waited for a moment, wondering what Bryce would choose. He looked between the two siblings as if curious to see what other weird things they'd get him involved in, but, to her surprise, he decided to stay. She tried to ignore the fact that he was her boss and just think of him as a friend so she could do justice to her upcoming parts in Eric's and her new movie.

Soon enough, she was able to forget he was there and really get into the part with Eric. He changed his words occasionally from what they had done over the years, sometimes putting in things from the last few months. Carrie thought he'd done one to embarrass her in front of Bryce, but she ignored it and kept going. She felt like she'd made the day a success when one of her responses to Eric's made Bryce actually laugh aloud.

And with Bryce getting into it, Eric couldn't keep a straight face and finish his lines, so Carrie finished for him, making the two guys laugh harder. It felt good to see Bryce relaxing enough from his stern bossy kind of personality into something that seemed more human and friendly.

When her character died a horrific and cheesy death, Carrie pretended the spirit of the woman was hungry and craving leftovers and excused herself from the room for a moment, telling Eric to carry on without her.

She heated some hot chocolate, grabbed a couple of napkins and spoons and a bowl of mini marshmallows, and returned to the living room to find Eric and Bryce talking with the movie still playing in the background, though the volume had been turned down. She listened in for a moment as the two talked about what Eric was doing in school, and she was surprised to hear him answer Bryce's questions.

Carrie hadn't heard where he wanted to go to college, as if that was even an option, but for some reason, he explained his plans to Bryce, and she was pleased to know he actually had a plan for after high school. She wasn't his mother, and neither one of them wanted to be like their father, or older brother. Though Bryce was like Shane in many ways, something about him freed Eric to open up and answer questions as well as ask some of his own.

She placed the hot cocoa on the coffee table in front of them and eased her way into the background, hoping to not disturb their conversation.

Bryce dropped a couple of marshmallows into his mug, but Eric took scoop after scoop until it threatened to overflow.

Bryce took a small sip, then spoke. "I think you've got the makings to do well in your art, but, though your talent is good, you could do with some training from some professionals. I could help get you some interviews and make a few contacts for you, but if you don't have a decent G.P.A., most schools would think twice about taking you. Talent will get you so far, but you have to show your reliability and your seriousness. Most schools look at your transcripts just as equally as they do your portfolio."

Carrie had told Eric the same thing, but the way Bryce had put it seemed to settle on Eric easier, and she could see him take the information and store it away instead of just arguing and dismissing it because it came from her.

I could kiss him for helping Eric like this.

The moment she thought of kissing him, she realized it wasn't just a peck on the cheek she longed to do. She wanted something more. Something that meant a lot more than an employee should be thinking about her boss. She took a sip of her hot chocolate and let the warmth settle in her chest just as the warmth she felt toward Bryce settled in her heart.

Chapter Thirteen

Bryce read the text from Carrie and excused himself from the man he was talking to. "I'm sorry, I have something I need to take care of. I'll have my secretary get the rest of this worked out."

Thanksgiving dinner at Carrie's house had been one of the most enjoyable evenings he'd spent in a long time. He'd jokingly told her he'd faked important texts to get out of uncomfortable situations. And though her text wasn't overly important — just to touch base and update on the things she'd accomplished for the upcoming artist gallery exhibit — he was relieved he could use her as an excuse to stop talking to this latest investor.

He wouldn't be able to meet with Carrie in person for another few days, and for some reason that bothered him. He'd gone over possible excuses to actually see her, but he knew her schedule at Carlson's was busy. The holiday season was overly rushed, especially with people trying to get the most out of the

Christmas gift-giving frenzy by getting their products in front of customers.

On top of that, she was still pulling double duty with her social media blitzes and getting his plans and events as trending topics for the local area. His non-profit, though initially funded by himself, was now the recipient of a fundraising event that was bringing in more money than he thought possible. All because of the plans and the way Carrie had presented it to the public.

Many companies were looking for charities to donate to so they could have a better tax write-off, and his plan for the youth programs was something a lot of companies were willing to help out with.

Though he hadn't expected to be able to get the theater and music programs going for at least a year, there was enough interest that he was sure they could get it started by late spring or early summer.

I don't want to make Howard upset, but I would love to steal Carrie away all to myself.

He paused a moment as that thought took hold on him in another way. No. He would keep it professional. He respected her too much to let anything happen between them. Besides, she needed someone more her age. Someone who would get her social references. Someone who would take her to do the kinds of things she liked. After the movie had ended, they'd played a couple of games of cards. They'd chatted easily with Eric and Carrie telling him about their childhoods. He hadn't wanted to leave, and that feeling of not belonging yet, still being on the outside, had dissipated for a while with them.

Bryce closed the door to his office and studied his long-term goals, none of which included falling in love. He would get his outreach program going strong and work on branching out in his gallery, finding new talent and bringing better artists to it. Then he would move on to his next goal, whatever it took to keep him too busy to develop a relationship.

***

"Once again, you've done the impossible," Bryce said. "I didn't think we could top last month's gala, but tonight I think we had almost half again what was here before. And it's two weeks before Christmas. How did you do it?"

Carrie took a slow breath. "Well, sculpting is a little different than oil paintings, but it's still a big draw to the right crowd. Besides, it's two weeks before Christmas, so people need to look for gifts for loved ones. There are lots of shoppers looking for unique, one-of-a-kind gifts that can't be bought at the corner store or even online."

Bryce nodded, thinking of the gift he'd gotten Carrie as a thank you for all the hard work she put into this extra job. She was good at it, and he paid her well, but he hoped to make her happy with this one small gift. Well, it wasn't really small, but he thought it would go well in her apartment.

He'd noticed one wall in the hallway that would be the perfect spot for the rainbow painting. He hadn't measured it, but he was a good judge of size when it came to where to hang a painting. And though it wouldn't completely match her decor, it wouldn't stand out either. It would fit well, he thought. But now he was almost unsure of whether he should give it to her or not.

Will she read too much into a gift like this? She said people came to art shows looking for one-of-a-kind gifts for the people they loved, but he could still give it to her as a token of his appreciation for all her help. He decided he would wait for a little bit, not mention it right away, since he didn't want her to connect the thought of gift giving and love at the moment.

Bryce shook his head, annoyed at himself for all this overthinking. He shouldn't be this worried about what the woman would think. He'd given gifts of this sort to his other employees before. His secretary always picked out her favorite artwork, and he got it for her as a gift on top of the holiday bonuses he sent out with the paycheck before the holiday.

"How are things at Carlson's?" Bryce asked.

Carrie shrugged. "We're holding our own. We stopped taking new projects in November so we could focus on the Christmas marketing season, but we still have so many things crop up that we didn't expect. Or the client has some last minute things that we have to tweak. They hear about some kind of competition going on, so have to one-up the other company. It's doable, but it keeps us on our toes."

"Is this work for me interfering?" Bryce asked.

"Not much. I did have to stay up late a couple of nights, but it's all good. I am relieved we only have a few more weeks of this rush. It will be good to relax a little after the holidays."

"You doing anything fun for New Year's?" He hoped she could get some vacation time in before the rush for Valentine's picked up. Howard Carlson had always said he was busy during the major holidays. Bryce might have to take things easy in February if he wanted to keep Carrie working for him. She had agreed to a few months' trial, and from what he could tell, things were going well with them.

He hadn't been demanding or bossy once since she'd told him off for it. Now that he knew what she expected, it wasn't that hard to work around her demands. She was worth it, of course. He only hoped she thought he was worth working for. He'd have to bring it up after the new year. It would be a little early still, given he had hired her at the end of October.

"I don't have any solid plans for New Year's yet. Do you have an event you need help with?" she asked.

Bryce looked up and met her eyes. *Does she think I'm asking her out?* If he was honest, he wanted to, but he didn't have any plans for New Year's either. He'd been invited to a party held by the city for some of the larger business owners, but he hadn't responded yet.

As he studied her beautiful eyes, so full of joy and newness, he really wanted to spend New Year's with her, even if it was just as business. "It's possible. I have an invitation to First Night and thought it would be a good idea to meet with the city council and mayor in a more relaxed setting. If you are available, I would love for you to be my plus one."

Carrie's eyes lost a little bit of their sparkle, and he wondered what he had said to make her lose it, but she nodded and smiled, bringing the light back to her expression. "I think I could manage that. Let me know what kind of help you'd like, and what type of event it is."

"Black tie, I'm sure."

Carrie sighed. "Darn it, I guess I'll have to get a new dress."

Bryce shook his head. "No, I'm sure something like what you've worn to these events will be fine."

Carrie rolled her eyes. "You really don't know women, do you?"

Bryce blinked, then Carrie laughed. She placed her hand on his arm and let it rest there for a moment. "You just gave me the perfect excuse to go shopping. Of course I'm going to buy a new dress."

Bryce smiled and placed his hand on top of hers, relieved she hadn't pulled her hand away immediately. "Well then, I'm glad I could oblige." He patted her hand then felt his neck get hot when he realized that action looked a lot like what his grandfather used to do. He pulled his hand away and took a step back. She probably thought he was a creepy old man. "Hopefully your Christmas bonus will help cover the cost of it."

"It'll help. Mr. Carlson was very generous this year. We've had a great year at the agency."

"I'm glad, but I meant the one for working here."

Carrie's eyes widened. "But I've only worked for you a little while."

Bryce waved that comment away. "Well, I am the cause of you needing to buy dresses like that in the first place. I should make sure you can get enough to keep you happy. Besides, you've more than earned it, and it will be more like a uniform or…" Bryce felt his neck get hot again. He was sounding creepier and creepier with everything he said.

"I don't know what to say, Mr. Thomson." Carrie spoke softly, and he wasn't sure of how she felt about what he'd said. "You are very generous, and I appreciate it." She shook his hand, and Bryce immediately felt the difference between her earlier light and innocent carefree touch and this more business-like expression.

He had done something to upset her, but he wasn't sure exactly what and decided he'd only dig himself into a deeper hole if he asked her right now. It was late; he still had some things to see to before he could leave for the night, and he decided against telling her about the painting. He would have it delivered to her apartment tomorrow and have some professional hangers put it on her wall.

He'd have his secretary contact her and schedule a time. That way, he wouldn't have to hear her response to his gift at first. He was sure she liked the painting, but after her unexpected response about the bonus, he would just give it to her when he didn't have to hear her reaction to it.

***

Carrie glanced back at Bryce as he spoke to his curator. The Christmas bonus would be fabulous, but she wasn't sure how she felt about taking it. She didn't want to sound greedy, and when she had mentioned buying a dress, she hadn't expected him to offer to pay for it. It seemed odd coming from her boss. Then again, he didn't have a lot of common sense when it came to women.

He was handsome, but he seemed so awkward around women it was no wonder he was single now. She didn't know much about his ex-wife and why they had split, but he wasn't pursued by all the ladies, as far as she knew.

Carrie drove home replaying the evening in her mind. She hadn't spoken to Bryce much until after the event. She was pleased with how he had interacted with his clients and the guests who'd come to see the artwork by the talented sculptor.

They had been so busy, playing host and hostess to all the visitors, that she hadn't had a moment to talk to him, other than in passing or when she introduced a guest to him. But she had felt his gaze on her often throughout the evening. And she'd wished more than once that they could be alone. He always had someone coming or going in his office or in the gallery when they met. The only time they'd ever had any privacy had been during Thanksgiving dinner, and he had seemed so different then that she wasn't sure what he was truly like. But, oh how she wanted to get to know him. And the fact that he had invited her to the New

Year's Eve party with the mayor was amazing. It wasn't an event that she'd ever expected to attend, and they would be there in a professional capacity as a connection to the arts alliance. And it would help her career with Carlson's as well as increase the exposure and reach of the youth program.

Chapter Fourteen

Carrie rolled over in her bed, reaching for her cell phone on the nightstand with her eyes still closed and fumbled to turn it on. "Hello?"

"Ms. Winters please." The voice on the phone sounded a little familiar to Carrie, but she was so groggy she wasn't sure she could place it.

"This is she."

"I have a package to be delivered to your address."

Carrie turned back over and tried to sit up, hoping that would wake her a little more. She peeked at the phone to see if the number had some kind of name attached to it.

The woman on the other end quoted Carrie's address. "Is this correct?"

Carrie rubbed her hand across her face. "Who is this?"

"My name is Isabell. I work for Thomson Gallery and have a delivery scheduled for you. The truck should be there between nine and eleven today. Will someone be home during those hours?"

Carrie looked at her clock. It was eight a.m. on Saturday morning, two days before Christmas, and if she'd had her way, she would have been sleeping during those hours. Her late night, helping with the finishing touches on a couple of commercials with Carlson's, had led to an ice cream and movie binge with Abby. "Yeah, I'll be here. What is it you said is being delivered?"

"I don't know the contents of the package. I only make sure the delivery can be completed." The sounds of typing on the other end reached Carrie's ears through the phone. "Have a wonderful holiday, Ms. Winters." Her voice sounded bright and professional, but soul-less at the same time. She hung up the phone without a response from Carrie.

That suited her just fine. She dropped the cell phone onto the pillow next to her and rolled over, wishing to go back to sleep, but she really didn't want to answer the door in her jammies. The fact that she'd spilled chocolate ripple ice cream on them in her funk last night and hadn't bothered to change was slightly embarrassing, more so if she answered the door to the delivery guy wearing them.

Of course, he'd probably just have her sign for it and leave.

Carrie showered quickly and wrapped her hair in a loose bun, sticking a small clip in it to hold it out of

144

her way while she did her makeup. She wanted to go shopping today anyway, and maybe going in the morning would help minimize some of the crowds, not highly likely on a Saturday so close to Christmas, but she wanted time to pick out a good dress for the New Year's Eve party.

She debated on waking Abby up, but decided to let her wake on her own. She'd be more likely to agree to go shopping with her to help pick out the right dress if Carrie didn't annoy her first thing in the morning.

She got a bowl of cereal and had just sat down to eat it when the doorbell rang. She peeked through the peephole to see the truck from the delivery company. It was only ten after nine. She opened the door to greet the bald man on her doorstep. "You guys are prompt."

"First delivery of the morning." He held up a clipboard. "Carrie Winters?"

She nodded.

"Sign here please."

She took the pen. "What is it?"

The man looked at the paper then at her. "Art."

"Who's it from?" Carrie asked. She hadn't seen anything on the form she'd signed that indicated who had sent it.

The man shook his head. "Don't know, but we have instructions to hang it." He waved to the guy in the truck. "This is the place. Bring it in."

Carrie watched as a long thin crate was pulled out of the back of the van, placed on a dolly, and wheeled to her front door. She stepped back and allowed the men to maneuver it up the few stairs and into her front room. As soon as they unhooked it from the cart, she examined the outer box, looking for some indication of who'd sent it.

"Do you have a place picked out for this?"

Carrie stared dumbly at the man. "How could I? I didn't even know this was coming. I still don't know who it's from or why it's been delivered here."

The second guy pulled out a packing slip. "Says it's an original work of art from the Thomson Gallery."

"Mr. Thomson sent this?" Carrie looked at the box. "There has to be a mistake. I'm his assistant. Maybe it should have been sent to his house, and my address was put on here instead."

The delivery guy shook his head as he examined the packing slip. "No mistake. It's addressed to a Ms. Winters with the instructions to hang it in the long hallway between the kitchen and the bedrooms." The guy pointed toward said hallway with a raised brow, and Carrie looked there as well. Nothing hung on the wall currently, and she'd occasionally wondered what to do with that spot, but the hallway was narrow, and putting a large painting there seemed like it would be odd and out of place.

Carrie's attention returned to the bald delivery guy who had unwrapped the package, and she gasped in surprise at the unveiled painting. It was the rainbow one she'd admired at the first gala, the one she'd been sitting in front of when Mr. Thomson joined her before she'd cut her foot on the champagne glass. *How did he know how much I'd loved that piece? And what possessed the man to give it to me?* It was one of the pricier pieces, well over two-thousand dollars. And to have it hanging in her apartment just seemed wrong.

"I can't keep this." Carrie shook her head. She turned to the men who'd just taken all the wrappings off the painting. "Wrap it back up and take it away."

The guy shook his head. "Can't. You already signed for it. The instructions say to make sure it's hung."

The bald guy pulled off an envelope from the back of the painting. "This is addressed to you."

Carrie took it slowly, not sure what to do. She loved this painting, and the thought of owning something so beautiful made her heart happy, but she didn't think she deserved something like this and was uncomfortable accepting a gift of that magnitude. She opened the envelope and read the handwritten note from the artist then noticed a second note behind it from Bryce.

Antone wanted to thank you for all the hard work and support you gave him through this event. To show his appreciation, he gave me a deal on this piece when he heard how much you admired it. I thought it would look nice in your hallway. Please accept it as a thank you for all your help getting things working smoothly.

~Bryce

Carrie read the note over again, as well as the sincere thanks from Antone, and smiled. It was nice to know she was appreciated. And since it had come from the artist more than from Bryce, Carrie decided she wouldn't send it back.

"We good to hang this?" one of the delivery guys asked.

Carrie nodded. "Yes. Let's see what it would look like in that hallway." She led them to the area and stood to the side as they placed it against the wall. She had them move it around, little by little, until she was satisfied it was in the perfect spot.

As soon as the guys started drilling holes in the wall to put in the hardware to hang the painting, Abby came out of her room, questioning what was happening. Eric never poked his head out of his room, and it didn't surprise Carrie at all. The kid could sleep through anything.

"Wow," Abby said. "Where did you get this?"

"It was a thank-you gift from Mr. Thomson and Antone. He's the artist who did the showing last month. Apparently, he was happy with the publicity and exposure and gave Mr. Thomson a discount on this painting."

Abby studied it. "It's interesting."

"Don't you like it?" Carrie asked. She flipped the hallway light on then off to study it in the different lights. She might have to get something to hang above it to bring out the colors the same way they had at the gallery.

"Yeah, I like it. It's just not something I would have picked out. But I think it looks good here."

"Good thing, 'cause there isn't anywhere else I could put something this size without rearranging a lot of furniture." Carrie wasn't sure if she'd want it in her room. It would make her think of Bryce too much, and that could be kind of dangerous.

The delivery guys cleaned up the packing stuff and left while Carrie and Abby studied the painting for a moment longer, then they moved into the kitchen and sat at the table, positioning themselves where they could still see the painting.

Carrie studied it while Abby got her morning herbal tea. As her roommate joined her at the table, Carrie tore her gaze away from the painting and tried to forget the man who had given it to her.

"I didn't know you and Bryce were that close," Abby said, taking a sip.

"We aren't," Carrie said.

"Right, all men give their employees expensive gifts."

Carrie stared at Abby. "It's not like that." She pulled the note from Bryce out of her pocket and handed it to Abby, who read it then set it down on the table as if that answered her question.

"'*I thought it would look nice in your hallway*?'" Abby said, raising a brow. "He's been here and knows you well enough to know you liked this painting. I think there is more to this relationship than you're admitting."

Carrie looked back at the painting. "I don't have a clue what goes on in that man's head. Sometimes he seems like he's checking me out, sometimes he acts like I'm a valuable member of his team, and other times he treats me like one of the teens in his outreach program."

She thought about how he had taken her advice and done so much better interacting with his clients. How he had ever managed to sell paintings before, she had no idea.

He was a contradiction in so many ways. Much different than any other guy she'd ever dated — not that she was dating him, but she didn't know how to act with him. And there were too many times she'd thought things could change between them, to go from professional and business to more intimate. She could stop working for him at any time if she wanted, and since this wasn't her full time job, just a bonus side job, she didn't worry about losing her income if things went wrong.

"You like him, don't you?" Abby asked.

"I'm not sure. Sometimes he drives me crazy. Other times, he's the sweetest and most patient and amazing man on the planet. I don't know what to think anymore."

"You know what I think?" Abby said, swirling her tea around in her mug. "I think you ought to see where this goes. You're smitten, I can tell. The way you talk about him and the work you two do together, you sound like the perfect match."

Carrie shook her head. "Doesn't matter what I think or even feel toward the man. Unless he gives me some indication this could go somewhere, I'm not going to make a move on him. He was here for Thanksgiving dinner and shook my hand goodbye, not even a kiss on the cheek. He spent more time talking to Eric than he did me once he came back from his date. Sure, we had a good dinner together, but we mostly talked about work. He's so private I don't think he'd ever open up about anything, and he certainly won't be making any moves on me."

"Then you make the move. Didn't you say you were going to the New Year's Eve party? We'll find you the perfect dress and get you all dolled up. Then when the time is right — like midnight — you make your move."

Carrie thought about it, and though the idea was scary, it also thrilled her. Bryce was so different than her usual dates, but none of the men in her social circles even interested her anymore. She hadn't missed going dancing or to the clubs with Abby when work interfered. Not even her surfing buddies were interesting anymore.

Though she usually looked forward to Christmas, this year wouldn't be as much fun since her mother was across the country with her new husband, and Eric had been spending more time with Kourtney than at home. It would be very simple and a time to relax from all the pressures of work since Mr. Carlson wouldn't have them come in over the next few days.

Bryce had told her he didn't want to be bothered during Christmas about anything dealing with the outreach program. There would be time again after the holiday, before they met for the New Year's Eve party, to discuss things for the mid-January event.

Chapter Fifteen

*B*ryce knocked on Carrie's door and waited for her to answer. He'd decided to take her out to dinner before the New Year's Eve party began and was glad the night was so clear. Of course, Southern California was well-known for its gorgeous weather, even into the winter. Where he'd grown up in Idaho would be covered in snow and ice by now.

When she opened the door, the first thing that caught his eye was her beautiful smile, framed with a deep red lipstick. Then her eyes drew his attention followed by her up-swept hair that revealed a delicate neck and sparkly earrings that could be diamonds, though they weren't overly large or gaudy, just enough to add a hint of style without drawing all attention away from the masterpiece in front of him.

"You found a dress to suit you?"

Carrie looked down, and he examined the midnight-blue dress she wore. It wasn't skin tight, but it accentuated her curves perfectly without making her look like she was trying to offer up everything to anyone interested in looking.

"Yeah, took a while to find one I liked, but this is it."

Bryce nodded. "Excellent choice. You look lovely."

"Thank you." Carrie peeked inside her clutch purse then tucked it under her elbow.

Bryce offered her his arm, and she placed her hand on the back of his then turned her head to peek back into the house. "I'm heading out, Eric. Have fun tonight. You have money for a cab, just in case?"

"Yeah, I've still got the cash you gave me an hour ago." Eric shook his head. "We'll be fine. I'm just going to hang out with some friends. We aren't gonna be drinking."

Carrie didn't move for a moment, just watched Eric, and Bryce wondered if there was something more she wanted to say to him. She nodded then waved before pulling the door closed and stepping outside with Bryce.

"You're worried about him?" Bryce asked.

"It's hard to forget what he has overcome. Last year he would have been out getting high. But he's really changed over the last few months. I think he wants to actually make something of his life now."

"That's good. He has a lot to offer the world. I hope he does everything he can to do so."

154

Carrie looked at him as they walked to his car. Bryce stopped at her door and opened it with one hand, not wanting to pull back the arm she still held.

She placed her other hand on his and gave it a gentle squeeze. "Thank you for your part in this. He's needed a good male role model. Our father isn't much of one, and our older brother is more of a control freak than a mentor. You've been something to Eric that he's needed in his life, and I really appreciate it."

Bryce nodded. It stung that she saw him as a father figure or an older-brother type person, but it was good to know how she saw him. "I'm glad I could help in whatever way. He's a good kid."

Carrie took her hands off him to slide into the car, and he felt the loss immediately. He walked around to his side wondering if he should change the subject or see where she would lead the conversation. She seemed in deep thought as he got in the car, so he remained silent as he started the vehicle and drove into town.

"Is Gerard's okay?" Bryce asked.

"Absolutely," Carrie said. "I've never been there, but have heard great things about it."

"It's a favorite of mine," Bryce said. He paused a moment. He could say something more but didn't know a safe topic. It was much better to think of her as an employee than as a woman. At least as her boss, he had more things to discuss.

As he contemplated what to say, Carrie saved him the trouble and brought up the youth program. "Eric is excited to show some of his artwork at your event. He's also been telling me about a couple of the projects some of the other kids have completed. Have you been to the rec center in the last few weeks to see the progress?"

Bryce shook his head. "Too many things going on. I had planned to stop by this Wednesday. How about you? Have you made sure all the projects are ready?"

"Yeah, I was there yesterday. We only have two youth who need a few more days to finish up. And the mentors have been creating projects too. I can't wait to let the public see what you've accomplished."

"I'm rather pleased with it, actually. It has turned out better than I expected, thanks to you."

***

Carrie talked about a few of the plans for work and what else needed to be done as Bryce drove them to the restaurant. He seemed distant, and she hoped the evening would improve. He probably had many things on his mind, especially with needing to convince the mayor to back his plan so they could get the city to help pay for some of the other events he wanted to get going. She knew Bryce could have paid a lot of it on his own, but it shouldn't be bankrolled completely by a private citizen.

With all the benefits coming to the community, it made sense that they should help fund it. Carrie's background in marketing would be helpful when it came time to actually pitch his ideas to the committee who'd make the final call on it, but having a good evening and schmoozing with some of those in a position of influence would help his cause.

That was probably why Bryce had invited her to the party. She was good eye candy as well as smart enough to judge the way people were feeling, enough that she could suggest ideas and help him with the wording on his pitch. He'd been effective at getting as far as he was now, but with a little bit of softening and some guidance from her, his influence had already improved.

She was good at what she did, and it was obvious Bryce knew that. It was only slightly disappointing to realize this was completely a business date, and nothing personal would arise from it. Abby had gone over a bunch of ways Carrie could make it more intimate and personal tonight, but most of those involved throwing herself at Bryce, and she didn't want to do that — especially in a public place where lots of people would be watching.

No, she would keep it to business and just enjoy the night with an intelligent man without worrying about him trying to invite himself back to her apartment. Tonight would already be much better than the last New Year's Eve.

Bryce pulled the car up to the front of the restaurant and got out to open her door as a valet approached the car. Bryce handed the guy his keys, took a valet parking ticket, and escorted Carrie into the restaurant before the cool evening air had a chance to chill her. She had thought about bringing a wrap but figured they'd be inside most of the time and had left it on her bed, not wanting anything to hide the dress she had finally settled on after trying on over a dozen.

The warmth of the building eased her nerves for only a moment before the romantic atmosphere made her question again why she was here with her boss. She glanced at Bryce, but could read nothing from his expression. If she didn't stop freaking herself out with every little thing, she was going to be exhausted before midnight ever came about. That was no way to celebrate the end of a good year and welcome in something new and hopeful. She decided from that moment on to just be herself and imagine she was with a friend. He wasn't her boss for the night, and he certainly wasn't her boyfriend, or anything of the sort. They'd had a great Thanksgiving dinner together. They could celebrate New Year's as well.

Once she relaxed, the meal was more enjoyable than she'd expected. They had a pleasant conversation without talking only about work things, and he hadn't tried to order for her.

By the time they finished eating and headed back to the car, Carrie felt hopeful about the rest of the evening. Bryce even looked like he was having a good time. They talked more in the car about things completely unrelated to work, and Carrie opened up a little about her hobbies and likes.

"You surf?" Bryce asked.

"Yeah." Carrie rubbed her wrist. "I haven't done it for a while. Been kinda busy, and the cast made that out of the question for weeks, but I'm looking forward to going out again soon."

"But it's winter."

Carrie grinned as he gave her a look like she was crazy. "The weather can be a little chilly, but the water is sometimes warmer in the winter because of El Niño and the ocean current patterns."

"Really?" Bryce asked.

Carrie nodded. "Have you never been in the ocean in the winter?"

Bryce shook his head. "Never had much interest in learning to surf once I moved out here. I've been too busy with work."

Carrie sighed. "If work keeps you too busy to enjoy a weekend at the beach or a chance to play in the ocean, you don't understand what life is about."

Bryce didn't respond, and Carrie hoped she hadn't offended him, but he finally spoke before she could panic about it too much. "I suppose you're right. Maybe I should make a trip to the beach. It's just not easy to make it fit into my schedule."

"Then tell your secretary you're taking a few days off. I'm sure the world can go on without you pushing things around for a moment."

"It's probably too late for me to take up surfing, but if I were to go to the beach, which one would be the best?"

Carrie shrugged. "Depends on what you're looking for in a beach. Do you want to see the sea lions, do you want to relax on a sandy beach and play in the waves, or do you just want to watch the sun set and ponder your next move in life?"

"I wouldn't know, maybe some of each."

"Then it doesn't matter which beach you choose. You'll get a little of all of it, depending on where you end up. It might do you good to just drive the coastline, see what the world has to offer."

"Good idea. I'll have to look into it."

"You should."

They drove for a few more blocks to reach the party, and another valet came to take the car while Bryce escorted her into the building. As soon as they entered, a waiter offered them each a glass of champagne. Bryce accepted, and Carrie decided she could handle one for the night — but she'd limit it to one. She wanted to celebrate, but would make sure she kept her wits with her.

Chapter Sixteen

Bryce had never been more thankful for having someone like Carrie by his side at an event like this. He would never admit that he felt completely out of sorts with his newfound money and his position of influence. He was happy to do what he could for the youth of the city, but he would never have a chance of making it this far if it hadn't been for Carrie.

She'd spent the night talking to everyone they met about how the program was going. Having had firsthand experience with the improvements in her brother's life, she was able to get the people who would have some influence on growing this program interested in helping out.

As the night progressed, the interactions became less about work and more about enjoying her company. Every move she made registered on his radar, mostly because she was close enough to brush up against him, time and time again. Her skin felt so smooth, and he longed to touch her until he finally gave in to the temptation and asked her to dance with him.

She blinked in surprise but accepted the invitation and placed her hand in his as he led her to the dance floor. He shifted her hand slightly as he turned to stand in front of her. She raised her other hand to his shoulder, and he placed his hand on the small of her back, very aware of the curve of her hips as she moved in time with the music.

Bryce swallowed and met her eyes. She stared into them and allowed him to take the lead in the dance. It was a slow dance but had enough movement to it that his ballroom dancing classes in high school would come in handy. She was fluid and had no difficulty keeping up with him. Her gaze never left his, but she smiled with joy as they glided across the floor. He pulled her closer, enjoying the sensations of her body as it pressed against his. Carrie's hand gripped his arm, and he turned again, releasing her just enough to transition her into a spin before bringing her back into him.

Her chest bumped against his, and her breath caught, then she laughed, completely doing him in. If they hadn't been in the center of the dance floor with dozens of people dancing around with them, he would have taken her face in his hands and kissed her right there. Fortunately, he had enough self-control to begin dancing again, but he didn't dare continue on the way he had been going.

He shifted into a more traditional dance form, keeping her right hand in his left, but he allowed his right hand to rest on her back again, forcing himself to stay high enough that he wasn't tempted to find out what her other curves felt like.

"Where did you learn to dance like that?" Carrie asked, the enjoyment in her voice obvious.

"Classes in high school."

"You took ballroom in high-school?" Carrie asked. "I always wanted to try that but didn't have time, being a cheerleader.

"Of course you were a cheerleader," Bryce said as another piece of her personality clicked into place. She was probably the most popular girl in the school, and he had been one of the boring geek types that took the ballroom dance class because his mom made him. Never in his life had he imagined he'd be able to woo a cheerleader. He was glad she hadn't known him in school.

He looked at her and was surprised to see the joy in her eyes had diminished. What had caused it? The song came to a close, and Carrie pulled away from him before the music ended completely. He missed her touch and was disappointed when the next song was more upbeat and not something that would allow slow dancing in the way he wanted to continue. He offered her his arm to escort her off the dance floor, and, though she seemed to hesitate for a moment, she placed her hand on his arm and followed him to a waiter with drinks and hors d' oeuvres.

Carrie didn't take another glass, but took a few of the bacon-wrapped appetizers and sighed with pleasure as she took a bite. "I wish I knew how to make these."

Bryce took one from the napkin she held out to him. The flavors were perfect together. "I don't think you'd have trouble coming up with something like this. If your Thanksgiving meal is any indication, you're very talented in the kitchen."

Carrie smiled and turned to speak with the waiter. "Do you know what's inside these?" She asked him little questions, and, though Bryce knew it wasn't flirtatious, he couldn't help feeling jealous that she was spending any time talking to someone beside him. He finished his glass of champagne and reached for another before the waiter was finished telling Carrie about the food.

Bryce turned his back to her, trying to get his thoughts in order.

***

Carrie smiled at the waiter and thanked him for humoring her as she pestered him with questions. She would probably never have a chance to make those delectable treats, but she could always dream. As she turned to find Bryce, the music changed, and another slow song came on.

She took a few steps to reach him. "Any chance I can convince you to dance with me again? I've never had so much fun dancing before."

Bryce's eyes filled with something Carrie thought for a moment looked like longing and desire, but he soon covered his emotions and nodded. "Sure."

This time, the dancing started stiffer than before, but as she kept up with him and anticipated some of the same kinds of moves he had done earlier, he seemed to relax, and she couldn't help giggling during some of the more exciting steps.

He twisted her around and held her close for a moment from behind as they swayed to the music, his arm across her chest and holding onto her hand as the other hand rested on her hip. She wished he would caress her arm and run his hands down her body, then blushed furiously as she realized what she was thinking. He pushed her gently away from him and turned her again until she was once more standing in front of him, this time facing him as he pulled her close, and prepared her for a dip that sent her pulse skyrocketing.

Her breath came fast and shallow as he stared into her eyes before straightening and pulling her to him, his arm behind her back, his palm splayed on her bare skin on the low-backed dress. Though the room was plenty warm, her skin shivered, and gooseflesh covered her arms as she stared into his deep eyes.

His breath wasn't nearly as labored as hers, but she knew he was affected as well. Carrie released her hold on his arm and placed her hand against his chest, feeling the pounding of his heart from the exertion of the dance. His face was still close to hers, as if he didn't want to pull away and stand completely straight.

She closed her eyes and took a slow, shaky breath, wanting more than ever for him to close the distance and kiss her. Her eyelids fluttered, and she opened them to see he was even closer than before, his own eyes heavy with desire.

Kiss me, she silently pleaded, holding as still as possible, afraid to break the spell.

The song ended and as another couple moved past, the woman laughed at something her partner said, and Bryce blinked then stood straighter, easing up on his hold of her, but not letting go completely.

Though there wasn't as much strength to their connection, it hadn't been severed completely, so

Carrie took hold of her courage and took Bryce by the hand. But before she could lead him off the floor, they were interrupted by one of the council members over the arts alliance who wanted to introduce Bryce to someone who had arrived late.

Carrie's heart thudded in her chest, but when Bryce didn't let go of her completely, keeping his arm around her waist, the butterflies inside lifted her up enough she felt like she was floating.

Chapter Seventeen

ryce was dying, and he loved every torturous minute of it. Carrie hadn't pulled away as they talked to the man who'd interrupted that incredible moment on the dance floor. Now they were walking off the floor and toward the lobby, with his hand on the small of her back feeling every little muscle move as she walked with him.

All rational thought had left him, and the only thing he wanted was to be alone with her where they wouldn't be interrupted by anyone. She was the only thing he wanted, and the intensity of his longing surprised him. He never thought he would allow a woman into his heart again after his wife left him for another man. But for Carrie, he was willing to open up.

As the music and the festive atmosphere permeated everything, his footsteps quickened, and Carrie picked up her pace. *Does she want to be alone with me as much as I want to have her to myself?* He could only hope, because he couldn't wait to taste her lips.

Bryce held the door for her, and she slipped through in front of him, but when her hand reached behind to grab hold of his before it left her back, his heart pounded in his chest, and he took a fast breath. He studied the mostly empty lobby, looking for the perfect place to take her, out of the way enough they could have the privacy they craved without making her panic or fear he was going to take advantage.

The lights were soft, lending the area a feeling of the holiday, and in a corner of one side of the room, a small Christmas tree with white lights and gold trim caught his eye. He led her there, and she came willingly, clinging to his hand with both of hers.

Words he would never dare say rolled through his mind, but he closed off the distracting thoughts and focused on the beauty before him. He lifted his free hand and tentatively touched her cheek. Carrie tilted her head and rested her face in the palm of his hand, her eye lids fluttering closed. Bryce took a slow step forward, lifting the hand that still held hers and bringing it between his chest and hers. She released his grasp and spread her palm flat against his chest, sending heat racing through to his core. His now free hand joined the other in cupping her face between his palms, and he used his thumbs to touch her bottom lip. Carrie's lips parted, and her eyes opened just a fraction, meeting his gaze and promising she would accept him.

Bryce groaned inside, knowing he couldn't fight this anymore, and he covered her mouth with his, tasting the sweetness she had to offer. He didn't want to attack her or overwhelm her with his desire, but when her lips moved against his and explored his mouth with an intensity almost matching his own emotions, the hold on his rational thinking disappeared, and he pulled her closer, deepening the kiss.

He had no idea how much time had passed, and he didn't care. The only thing that existed at this time was Carrie, and he wished there were no responsibilities in life. Nothing that would mean he would have to let her go or take her home. He wished for the completeness he felt with her. Though he had thought he'd known what love was when he married the first time, this all-consuming emotion tied to the woman in his arms was like an inferno compared to smoke.

He pulled back, reluctantly putting an end to the kiss, but Carrie kept her arms around his shoulders and rested her forehead against his neck, her deep breaths sounding as if she had as much trouble catching her breath as he did. He stood there, not knowing what to say, and wished she would step in and tell him how to handle this new situation he'd found himself in, but she didn't speak either, just kept hold of him. He was grateful for the opportunity to try to gather his wits.

***

Carrie didn't know exactly how this had all happened, but she didn't want to let go of Bryce and meet his eyes. She had never intended to seduce him, even with all of Abby's advice and suggestions. She replayed all their interactions throughout the evening, wondering if she had somehow done it anyway, but she couldn't think of a conscious effort toward seduction. When he'd held her as they danced, and she felt him open up to her on the floor, she'd wanted that kiss more intensely than she'd ever felt before with any guy.

When what she thought would be their first kiss ended with the interruption, she had been disappointed, but he hadn't let go of her, and she knew she would welcome whatever came. Enough so that she followed him out to the lobby and hid in a corner to make out.

His arms were still around her, holding her tenderly without expectations or demands of more, yet she wanted more. She lifted her head, intending to step back a little, but as she loosened her hold on him, he seemed to act reflexively, and his arms tightened. Carrie brought her hands down from where they'd stopped on his shoulders and allowed them to sneak into his suit jacket and around his warm back as he leaned down and kissed her again.

Her heart soared, and she allowed herself to fall hard for the man.

They stayed in the embrace for a few moments before the sounds of music from the ballroom caught her attention as someone opened the door. Carrie reluctantly pulled back, and Bryce released her but took her hands in his.

"Will you dance with me?" he asked, his voice raspy with what she thought was desire. She nodded numbly, tucked her elbow under his arm, and practically floated into the room, falling into step with him as soon as they reached the dance floor.

The evening flowed between dancing and stealing kisses until the clock struck midnight; then, while the other party goers celebrated with more drinks and dancing, Carrie and Bryce secreted themselves in a dimly lit corner at an empty table and talked of everything under the sun between more kisses and hand holding.

When it was time to head home, Bryce asked her to drive since he'd had a few drinks, and Carrie's admiration for him grew. He had obviously gotten over his issue with the accident and knew how she felt about drunk drivers, so even though he wasn't completely inebriated, he was impaired. She felt better knowing he wasn't a control freak in every aspect of his life.

He gave her his address, and she drove to his house, wondering what to do if he invited her in.

***

Carrie closed her door after the taxi dropped her off. She reflected on the difference of this date from the last time she'd taken a cab home from a drunk guy's house. Though the situation was similar, she had completely different feelings toward Bryce — respect and admiration for sure, but a growing feeling similar to love had slowly crept up as well.

She turned on the lamp on the end table to help her through the apartment and saw signs that Abby was home. She checked her roommate's door and was happy to see it cracked a bit. Abby was alone, and, through the door, Carrie could see the glowing light of a cell phone.

Carrie knocked softly on the door and Abby's voice invited her in.

"How was the party?" Carrie asked.

Abby shrugged. "A bunch of drunk, handsy-feely guys and just as many drunk chicks hanging all over them. You didn't miss much. How was yours?"

Carrie sighed, and Abby sat up higher against her headboard. "That good? Tell me everything." She patted the spot on her bed, and Carrie kicked off her shoes then lifted the top comforter to slide underneath in order to spill everything to her best friend.

Abby squealed in delight as Carrie described each agonizing detail leading up to that kiss.

"I told you he was interested in more than just an assistant," Abby said when Carrie had finished.

"I guess you were right, though I still can't believe it happened. And he was so great tonight, kissing me a couple more times when we got to his place, but we stayed in his car while we waited for my taxi to arrive. He said he didn't want things to move too fast and was worried about inviting me inside."

Abby sighed. "And such a gentleman, darn it." She giggled when Carrie pushed her shoulder playfully.

"I thought it was perfect. I would hate for things to move too fast. This all came about so suddenly tonight that I think we'll be better off to take it easy."

Abby nodded. "I think you're right. I'm so excited for you though. He's a much better catch than all the guys you've been with in the past. And he's solid, secure, and sexier than anyone I know."

Carrie sighed with joy. "I know. He looks so good in his suits. I'm almost ashamed to think I gave him the advice that he needed to wear something besides suits."

"Shame on you," Abby said, giggling.

They talked late into the night, and Carrie loved dreaming about what might be possible in her relationship with Bryce. He would be so good for her, and Eric would be ecstatic when he heard she was dating Bryce since he looked up to him so much.

Chapter Eighteen

ryce woke up with a mild headache and a feeling of joy after the evening he'd spent with Carrie. He wished he was waking up next to her, but though he wanted her desperately, it would be better to go slowly. He'd gotten involved with Margery so quickly that they hadn't really had a chance to learn each other's personalities and quirks. That relationship had soured too fast for him to want to repeat anything.

He took a couple of aspirin then a long hot shower, hoping to speed up the hangover recovery, and debated as to what he should do next. The way things had progressed the night before had surprised him. He had often thought of what it would be like to kiss her, but he hadn't consciously planned to do it that night — well, maybe a quick celebratory kiss at midnight — but when he'd held her close as they danced, he knew he was in trouble.

She was his employee, and he hoped she wouldn't be upset with him for crossing that boundary. He had been slightly drunk, not to the point he could blame it all on the alcohol, but he wasn't fully aware of everything he was doing. The feelings of the moment had taken over his senses, and he'd enjoyed it all.

But in the bright morning, he had begun to regret his actions. She was ten years younger than he, and as she'd told him of all the things she liked to do — like surfing, and biking, and hiking — he realized their interests were so different.

Sure, she enjoyed the arts, but he was so boring that she would more than likely resent the way he'd hold her back. Not to mention the fact that he had asked her to drive him home as if he were incapable of taking care of her. Bryce shook his head, disgusted with himself for his lack of planning. He should have hired a driver for the night so she wouldn't have had to take a cab home. She probably thought he was a jerk, and he'd just made out with her in the car like a horny teen.

He would have to be more careful when he saw her next. They would be meeting at the end of the next week to go over all the finalization of the youth program art exhibits.

Bryce brushed his teeth and debated on shaving then decided against it. When the headache was gone, he'd go work out. He stopped that thought when he realized there would be too many people starting out their New Year's resolutions at the gym in the morning.

Maybe he'd go for a run instead. He took a long drink of water and stepped outside into the cool morning air. He'd warm up soon enough and began his stretches then started at a slow jog to test his head. When he was sure he could handle it, he picked up the speed.

He allowed the pounding of the asphalt to distract him from thoughts of Carrie, but she soon found her way into his mind again. He ran harder and focused on keeping his breath steady. It worked until he had to turn around and head back to his house. As he ran up the long driveway, he caught sight of his car where they'd made out in the front seat. He had longed to be in the back of the car with Carrie, but it was a good thing there'd been a gearshift between them, forcing him to maintain some kind of distance.

He felt disgusted with himself for taking advantage of her like that.

As he entered his house, he picked up his phone and saw he'd missed a call from Carrie. She'd left a voicemail, and Bryce hesitated before pressing play.

Her voice was light and sweet, sounding happy and flirtatious, and he wanted to hit the button to call her back but decided against it. He needed time to sort this all out. She needed time to come to her senses. Bryce wanted her to realize, just as he did, that this couldn't work between them. He needed her as his hostess and press assistant, not his girlfriend or lover, no matter how much that idea appealed to him.

He erased the voicemail, knowing if he kept listening to her repeat what a good time she'd had last night and that she wanted to see him as soon as possible, he would give in.

He took another shower and when he got out, there was a text.

Carrie: Call me.

Bryce forced himself to leave the phone alone and instead focused on the work he needed to do. He'd made some good progress with the city council members over the arts and knew their hope for getting the city to fund some of these events was possible.

It was all thanks to Carrie, and he once again felt ashamed of taking advantage of her. She was too important to the community-outreach program for him to mess things up with his feelings for her.

***

Carrie stared at her phone. She'd already called him and left a message once, then sent a couple of texts. She was beginning to feel like a desperate woman who'd over-read the excitement of her date. *What's going on?* Last night, the world had seemed perfect, but today, it was like a completely different planet.

Eric dragged himself out of bed at noon and peered at her with heavy eyes. "What?"

"Morning, sleepy head. How was your night?"

Eric just nodded as he yawned. "Good. I creamed Tony in his games, then the girls showed up, and we watched some movies."

"Sounds fun. What time did you get in last night?"

"Two-thirty." He looked at her with one brow raised. "What about you? I made it back before Abby and you."

"Yet I woke up before you and even had breakfast and my morning run."

"So what time?"

Carrie smiled. "Four."

"Alone?"

Carrie rolled her eyes. "Of course."

"Disappointed?" Eric asked.

"Ew, Eric. Stop pestering me about stuff like that. It's kinda gross coming from my brother."

"Whatever. I can tell something happened. You're practically glowing. So either tell me, or I'll make assumptions based on my imagination."

"We just danced and kissed, nothing more. So get your mind out of the gutter."

"Mm-hmm, I'll bet." He grabbed a bowl out of the dishwasher and a spoon from the drawer, then poured himself some cereal and milk. "So what are you going to do with all his money?"

Carrie rolled her eyes. "I'm not going to get his money. There isn't anything really serious between us. Things are just starting out, so don't go all weird on me."

"Well, I know someone who could use a car when you start feeling generous."

"Dream on," Carrie said.

"Oh, I will." He took another spoonful and then met her eyes. "All joking aside, I'm happy for you. He's a pretty cool guy. I hope things work out."

Carrie smiled. "Thanks. Me too." She left the room, looking at her phone once again. The longer it took without an answer to her call or text made her worry she'd read too much into everything. But, with the way they hadn't been able to get enough of each other last night, she knew she was overreacting.

He was probably busy and would call her back later tonight.

Chapter Nineteen

By Friday morning, Carrie was seething. She'd called him twice more, once as a girl wondering where the guy she'd had such a wonderful date with had disappeared to, and the second as an employee trying to make sure she knew what he needed her to do with the next event on the calendar. She'd contacted his newest artist, and the woman had questions that Carrie had to get approval for before giving a response.

He hadn't answered her texts either, and she had wondered for a moment if something had happened to him, enough so that she'd driven past his house. No one was home. She had called his personal secretary, who oversaw the actual gallery. She assured Carrie that Bryce was alive and well, but busy in his office and had asked not to be disturbed.

Carrie gave Tonia the information from the artist. "I need the answer before the end of the day. The artist needs to know how many prints to order, and tonight is the last day to put the order in."

"I'll make sure he gives you the answers," Tonia said. "Is there anything else I can help you with?"

Carrie bit her lip and contemplated leaving another message. "No, that will be all. Oh, wait. I need to know if he still wants me to meet at his office on Tuesday evening next week."

"I'll find out and let you know," the secretary said.

"Thanks," Carrie said softly as she hung up the phone. So, the man was still alive, but at the moment she wished for all kinds of bodily harm to come upon him. *How can he ignore me like this?*

She forced the man out of her mind so she could work on the client accounts with Carlson's Ad Agency. Now that the Christmas rush was over, they were heading into Valentine advertisements, then, after that, things would slow down a little.

After sending updates, emails, consulting bills, and proposed advertising packets to the many different clients on her list, she headed to the breakroom. Madison Perry-Koholohini was pulling a dish out of the microwave and must have seen something in Carrie's eyes because she set the bowl down and moved closer to her.

"What happened?"

Carrie took a slow breath, not sure she wanted to explain her stupid love life, but still not willing to hold it all in. Maybe Madison could offer her a different perspective, because every conversation with Abby had left her more confused than ever.

Besides, Madison had worked with Bryce before, so she knew him a little better than Abby, who only had the observations from a distance at one of the gallery events.

"Can I ask a question?"

"Sure," Madison said. She turned, opened the breakroom fridge, and pulled out two cold Dr. Peppers. She offered one to Carrie.

"Thanks." Carrie popped the lid and took a long drink, trying to think of the best way to bring up her troubles. She decided to be completely blunt and honest. "You know I work for Bryce Thomson on his outreach program, and assist him with his art gallery, right?"

"Right."

"So on New Year's, we went to First Night and had a good time — and not just as coworkers. Things turned more personal. We danced and even kissed."

Madison smiled and opened her mouth as if to congratulate her, but she stopped when Carrie raised her hand to indicate she wasn't done.

"Thing is, he hasn't called me, or even returned my calls. Personal or work-related." Carrie fidgeted with the soda can. "Nothing happened besides a few kisses — fabulous kisses — but we didn't cross the line anywhere, as far as I know. And now he's completely ignoring me."

Madison shook her head and clicked her tongue. "That's no good."

"I know. But I don't know what to do about it. I thought something special had happened, and it's not like I was going to rush things or demand anything serious, but the fact that he's completely shut me out and ignored me over the last few days is awful."

"Maybe something came up, and he had to leave town for work reasons?"

Carrie shook her head. "I checked with his secretary to get some information about our projects, and she says he's there at the office, just too busy to take any calls. But from the way she answered the phone and from what she said when she knew it was me, I think he told her to not put my calls through."

"Strange," Madison said. "I don't know what to tell you. What are you going to do?"

Carrie shook her head. "I don't know. I was hoping you might have some suggestions, but just knowing you don't think I'm over reacting or taking things wrong helps. I guess I'll have to wait until I hear from him. His secretary should be getting back with me today about my questions, and she'll let me know if we're still on for our meeting next week."

"Good luck. Let me know if you need me to take some of the accounts off your hands for a bit. I know you've been working double-time, especially with this crazy holiday season. And since most of the pitches and client acquisitions have slowed down a bit lately, I do have a little free time."

"Thanks, Madison. I really appreciate that. For now, I think I'm covered, but depending on how the project goes next week, I'll let you know if I need some help."

Madison patted Carrie on the shoulder. "I'm sorry things are so weird with Mr. Thomson. I hope he puts his head back on straight and contacts you, at least to let you know where things stand. There's nothing worse than not knowing where things are and what move to make next. Better to just get the answer, no matter how painful it is."

Carrie sighed. "I know. It's not like things were serious or anything, but I'm really confused, given how New Year's Eve went. I want answers. He owes me that at least." Carrie lifted the Dr. Pepper. "Thanks for the help and for this. I think everything is better with a Pepper."

Madison smiled. "Amen."

Carrie returned to her office and worked more on the accounts until they were all done. She stared at her phone. She turned away from it and checked her office email, then her personal email, but there was nothing in there to answer the question that kept plaguing her.

Since everything with Carlson's was caught up, she figured it would be okay to work on the youth outreach program and sent some emails and texts to the mentors who were supervising the projects. The two they weren't sure on had made a lot of progress over the last few days and would probably be ready to display theirs on time.

She got as far as she could without input from Bryce and grumbled under her breath. She opened a new email document and sent him the information that way. Maybe eventually she'd get a response. If she didn't hear back from him by Saturday afternoon, she'd send him a letter of resignation, because she could not work this way.

While Carrie cussed Bryce out for his stupidity, her phone finally rang. It wasn't him, but she thought the number was probably his secretary. *Maybe now I'll get some answers.*

"Carrie Winters."

"Ms. Winters, this is Tonia. I have the information you requested."

Carrie grabbed a pen and took notes on the answers for the artist then waited to hear what else Tonia had to say. "Mr. Thomson apologizes for his schedule, but he won't be able to take your calls for a few days. He did say that meeting Tuesday would work, and that he's looking forward to moving on the youth program exhibit."

Carrie pressed her lips together to prevent herself from letting out her frustration on the secretary.

"Is there anything else, Ms. Winters?"

"No, thank you, though." She pinched the bridge of her nose. "I need to speak with Mr. Thomson in person, but if he isn't available until Tuesday, I'll give him the information then."

"Very good. Have a wonderful afternoon, Ms. Winters." The secretary hung up, and Carrie pressed her phone off.

"Well, at least I can move on a little." She mentally ticked off her to-do list to make sure she had everything done that she needed, and when she realized she was actually caught up, she picked up her phone and sent a text to Eric.

Carrie: You up for a trip to the beach this weekend?

Eric: Absolutely.

Carrie: Be packed and ready to go in an hour. We'll get a motel too.

Eric: Awesome! Can I bring Kourtney?

Carrie: If she's ready to go when I get home. See if Abby wants to come too.

Eric: Will do.

Carrie breathed a slow, cleansing breath. This would be just what she needed. Time in the ocean always made things better.

When she got home, it took Carrie less than twenty minutes to get her surf gear ready. Eric and Kourtney had the boards strapped to the top of her car on the racks by the time she hauled her bags outside and shoved them in the trunk.

Abby couldn't make the trip on such short notice, so Carrie hugged her goodbye and got in the car while Eric and Kourtney sat in the back seat together. She turned to look at them. "I'm gonna lay down the law now. Kissing… I'm fine with. Hand holding is just perfect, but I'm kinda ticked about a guy, so if you two get disgustingly gross, I'm kicking you out, and you'll have to find your own way home. Got it?"

They glanced at each other and nodded.

Carrie narrowed her eyes. "And though we're sharing a motel room, you two are not sharing a bed. Understand?"

"We weren't planning on it," Eric said.

His girlfriend nodded as if it just dawned on her that they were spending the next two nights together.

"Good. Now let's go have some fun." She switched her phone to *Do Not Disturb* and tuned her music to her playlist with very little romance music and turned the volume up. There was nothing worse than getting a call or text in the middle of her favorite song.

As she drove to the beach, she replayed the conversation she'd had with Bryce about surfing, and how he'd never spent much time at the beach in all the time he'd lived in California. If he had never made the effort to enjoy the beauties of the world they lived in and only watched from a distance, she wasn't sure she wanted to be involved with someone like him anyway.

She pulled into the parking lot of the motel where they had reservations, glad it wasn't the busy season, and that they'd had vacancies. This one was close enough to the beach they could walk there in the morning and get some good surfing in before most people woke up.

She was lucky the weather was cooperating with her desire to get away. If she'd had to stay at home fretting about not getting a return phone call, she'd probably have done something she'd regret, like stalking Bryce and showing up at his house, demanding answers.

After stepping out of the car, she paused a moment to breathe in the fresh ocean air. Though she loved her job and where she lived, every time she returned to the beach, she wished she could live there and go out surfing whenever the fancy struck her. At least she was close enough she could do a quick trip like this.

They checked in, and Carrie climbed beneath the sheets, sliding over enough to give Kourtney room to join her on the queen-size mattress. Eric would have his own bed. At least, she hoped it would remain just him, but she wasn't going to push. She'd stated her expectations; it was up to him to make the decision on how to live his life.

"I'm heading out first thing. You two joining me?" Carrie asked.

They nodded and prepped for bed while Carrie set the alarm on her phone. She checked for messages and was once again disappointed there was nothing from Bryce. She needed to get over that soon. He wasn't worth it, and she didn't have to put up with his childish behavior.

Chapter Twenty

*B*ryce paced his office. He was going to be in trouble with Carrie for ignoring her calls, but didn't feel equipped to talk to her that first morning. He couldn't believe he'd allowed himself to get inebriated enough he'd kissed her. The way he felt about her concerned him. He could probably have been forgiven for not calling her back that first day, but when he missed her calls the second day, he should have at least sent her a text that night. Instead, he'd researched his newest upcoming artists and had sat down on his couch and fallen asleep until the wee hours of the morning.

By Friday night, he'd cleared his Saturday schedule, managing to catch up enough that he decided to call her. Maybe they could meet in the morning. *Carrie will probably be ticked, but I have to talk to her before Tuesday.* One, because he needed to answer a few of her questions, and two, because he realized he missed her.

He'd spent too much time thinking of the way she'd felt in his arms as they'd danced, and the kisses she'd shared with him had melted a little of the ice around his heart. He wanted to see her and enjoy the warmth her personality radiated.

Originally, he hadn't cared if she shared it with others, but after seeing what it was like, now he wanted to claim it all for himself.

The phone went right to voicemail. He hesitated for a moment, thinking he should say something, but he'd always felt awkward leaving messages. He hung up the phone and opened up the text messages she'd sent. It would sound incredibly stupid to type the way he felt about her in a message after looking at the professional way she'd sent him the questions and updates.

He read through them, wondering which ones his secretary had answered and figured most of them had probably been addressed. He didn't want to seem like a micromanaging boss, so he decided against responding to her questions. Bryce looked at the screen for a moment, wishing he knew what to say to her. He'd missed his chance and regretted not contacting her earlier.

It was sad to admit it, but he honestly felt like he needed to hire someone like Carrie to guide him through the social interactions with someone like Carrie.

She knows me better than anyone else. Will she forgive me for this or hold it against me since I should be able to talk to an employee?

The phone's screen went black since he had spent so long staring at it. It wouldn't do him any good anyway. What he wanted to say wouldn't come across in a text. Until he could actually talk to her in person, he'd be better off just waiting. He'd try again in the morning and see if there was a chance she'd like to go out for lunch or even dinner. He fantasized for a moment about taking her to a place they could dance, but thought that wouldn't be the best option.

Bryce slipped the phone into his pocket and finished taking care of the last few items he needed to do before heading home for the weekend. He hoped she'd answer in the morning, since now that it was past nine, he didn't think it the best time to try calling her again.

When he finished eating the dinner his housekeeper had left him in the fridge, he reflected again on his loneliness. After Margery had left him, he really hadn't cared about the emptiness of his house, but now the buzz from the refrigerator's motor and the sound of the fork clinking on his plate only punctuated his isolation. Nothing on television looked good, and he wasn't in the mood to pick out a movie from his collection. No, it would be best to go to sleep and mentally prepare himself for what he'd say when he called her in the morning.

***

Carrie woke at six a.m. and grabbed a granola bar from the food she'd brought. She didn't want to eat too much but needed something to give her a boost of energy before she surfed. She slipped on her wetsuit as Eric went into the bathroom to prep for the day. Kourtney pulled on her wetsuit, and Carrie offered a granola to her.

"You ready for this?" Carrie asked.

The girl shrugged. "I've never surfed in the winter, but Eric says it's great. Is the water really warmer than in the summer?"

"I think so," Carrie said. "The air is cooler for sure. That's why I like the wetsuit, but with the water currents shifting, the water is often warmer."

"Nice," Kourtney said.

Eric walked out of the bathroom with his wetsuit on but not zipped up all the way. His tattoos didn't look nearly as weird on him as they had the first time she'd seen them. He was growing up, and he seemed happy with Kourtney. Carrie hoped things would continue to go well for him. It was nice to see him enjoying life, living it in a way that wasn't likely to end up with him either in jail or dead.

The outreach program had been a good thing, and Eric had for sure benefited from it, even in the few months he'd been involved.

Thoughts of Bryce made her frown, and she glanced at her phone. She vowed to ignore him for the weekend. She could discuss work stuff on Tuesday, and if things between them had changed too much to be comfortable after New Year's Eve, then she'd figure out where to go next.

Kourtney gave Eric a granola, and they grabbed the stuff they'd need at the beach and headed out the door. The sand was chilly but not bad. Carrie hoped the water wouldn't feel too cold, but she wasn't going to let that stop her. She hadn't been in the ocean for months. Her wrist had healed, and she had been so glad to get rid of that horrid cast not long after Thanksgiving.

She walked ahead of Eric and Kourtney, and, when the water covered her feet, she took a quick breath and pushed on, shifting her board a little higher to get a good grip on it before walking out into the waves. They weren't the largest she'd ever seen, but they would do for a warm up.

There was only one other surfer in the water, and his buddy sat on the beach on a blanket, watching. *This will be the perfect way to relax. I can use up all this pent-up energy and just have a good time.* The workweek would come soon enough, and she'd get back to let Mr. Thomson know she wouldn't be working with him past the end of this current project. She just didn't want to deal with stuff like this, and with the way she had started to fall for him on New Year's Eve, Carrie didn't want to let her heart get beat up any more. It would be best to end it as soon as possible, before it could even start, if she was honest with herself.

She lay on the board and paddled herself out past the smaller waves to get in position for the ones that would carry her back onto the beach. As she worked her way out, she let herself forget the man and instead enjoyed the feel of the water as it embraced her arms each time she paddled. The wind wasn't bad at all, and the wetsuit kept her from feeling any discomfort from the water temperature.

Carrie smiled as Eric and Kourtney worked their way out. They looked so happy, and Carrie was glad she could be a part of this for them. Yes, coming to the beach was the best thing she could have done this weekend.

She watched the water and spotted the beginnings of a wave. It formed in just the right way, so she lay down on her stomach and paddled forward to get in position. As the water hit the back of the board, she jumped up to her feet, gaining her balance easily, and allowed the wave to carry her.

The wind blowing past her helped clear her head, and she enjoyed the simple pleasure of the ocean.

***

The weekend was exactly what Carrie needed. They had surfed all Saturday morning then headed back to the motel to sleep and relax. Later they watched a movie, eaten at a cute little shop near the beach, then returned for more surfing in the afternoon before crashing for the night. Sunday morning, they went surfing just long enough to get in some great waves before hurrying back to the motel in order to shower before checkout.

"I'm not in a rush to get back home," Carrie said as they got in the car. "What about you?"

"My parents want me home for dinner," Kourtney said.

"Okay," Carrie said. "Mind if we take a detour though? I've got a place I want to see since it will give me an idea for one of my clients at work."

"That's fine with us," Eric said. He took Kourtney's hand and rested his head on her shoulder as if planning to nap the whole way.

Carrie turned her phone on, and when she saw that she had never switched it back to accepting calls, she realized she hadn't thought much about Bryce since Friday night — except for the times she saw his face as she closed her eyes… or when she watched the movie and remembered when they had invited him over for Thanksgiving dinner… or when she thought of him talking to his clients or artists… or the way some of the kids at the youth program had started to warm up to him. But, she had managed to keep thoughts of those kisses out of her mind.

She turned her phone back on to accept calls, since she might have something she needed to be aware of before Monday morning.

A few alerts *pinged* her phone, and she looked them over… a few texts from Abby checking to see if they were having a good time… a call from one of her clients with Mr. Carlson… a return call from her stylist saying she was back from vacation and ready to take her when she needed…

And a missed call from Bryce.

But there was no message, and he hadn't sent her any texts either. She scrolled through the missed calls and saw one was from late Friday night and one was on Saturday morning. *Why didn't he leave a message?*

She knew it shouldn't bother her too much, but hadn't they worked enough together that he should know she could be professional? *At least about work?* Couldn't he make up an excuse about needing to tell her something to do with the project they had coming up? *Ugh, I just want to shake some sense into the man. I will not be his assistant when it comes to a relationship.*

She listened to the few messages and knew they could wait until she got back home, then turned her music on without blocking any calls. If Bryce called today, she wanted to be able to answer. *But what would she say, and did she really want to have an audience if he did?* If she was lucky, Eric would fall asleep followed soon by Kourtney, since they hadn't even started driving yet, and both of them looked almost out already.

Yet as she drove, the phone never rang. She tried not to let it bother her, but the more she thought about it, the more annoying it became, and by the time she got home, she was more upset with Bryce than when she had left. She unpacked her gear and stowed away her surfboard in the closet, then went to take a long hot bath.

She turned the water on, poured in her favorite bath oils, and grabbed her deep-conditioning treatment for her hair. She slipped out of her clothes and, just as she put one foot in the water, Bryce's ringtone on her phone chimed. Carrie pulled her foot out and wrapped her large towel around herself before picking up the phone.

"Hello?"

"Is this Ms. Winters?" Bryce's voice came through, but with the sound of the water running,

Carrie couldn't decipher his mood. She quickly shut off the water.

"This is Carrie," she said, hoping that by using her first name, things could be a little less formal, and she could find out where he was in his own emotions toward the two of them.

"I'm sorry. Are you busy?" Bryce asked. "I can call back later."

"You're fine," Carrie hurried to assure him. She didn't want to run the risk of him hanging up before she figured out where things were with them. Her heart rate had increased with nerves, and she mentally told herself to relax. She didn't need to be nervous. *I'm a grown woman, not in high school anymore. I don't have to freak out about being kissed. Who cares if it was all for fun and meant nothing to him?*

Even though she tried to convince herself things would be fine, whatever way they went, she knew it was a lie. Just hearing his voice on the other end made her remember the kiss and how it had been a perfect ending to the year. She still admired him for all the good he did in the community as well as with her own brother. She hoped that she could be a part of his life as more than just an assistant.

Bryce spoke, and Carrie hung on the words. "I wanted to apologize for not contacting you sooner. Things got busy at work. I do hope my secretary has given you the answers you needed."

"Yes, Tonia has been very helpful." Carrie paused, not sure if she should say more or if she should let him lead the conversation. She didn't want to pressure him into anything. And though she was usually very assertive in their interactions, she didn't want to push him away, not now when he'd finally called.

She had never felt this confused and out of sorts talking to a man, not since she'd been in early high school.

"I'm looking forward to meeting with you on Tuesday, though," Carrie said. "I think things will work smoothly for your event. Did you get the details I sent?"

"Yes." Bryce sounded distracted.

Carrie worried that talking business with him after saying she wanted to see him on Tuesday had made him think she was only interested in a business-type relationship.

"I don't want to keep you long, just wanted to touch base with you," Bryce said, and Carrie's heart sunk. "I'll see you on Tuesday. Goodnight, Ms. Winters."

Bryce hung up before she could think of any way to keep him on the phone. She had lost her chance to tell him what a fun time she'd had on New Year's, though she'd already told him in the text and phone call. And he'd never even replied. Since he hadn't brought up anything, Carrie decided he must not want to think about it.

She sighed deeply. It hurt, but she wouldn't let it affect her any longer. She'd pined about this for long enough. She was an adult. They had enjoyed a few kisses, but come Tuesday, she would be back to her professional self. She would be the assistant he needed until this project was done, then cut ties with him and turn all of her attention on her job with Carlson's Ad Agency. She had enjoyed the extra income, but now that she'd payed off the rest of her bills from the accident and would be able to pay off her replacement car by the time this event was over, she could go back to her regular job.

Carrie turned her music on again, hoping her choice of romance songs wouldn't turn around and bite her, and dropped her towel before slipping into the water. The temperature was perfect, and she sank into it until it covered her face, holding her breath for as long as her lungs would allow before surfacing and letting the tears leak out, camouflaged by the water.

I don't need him. She took a long breath. *But oh, how I want him.*

Chapter Twenty-One

*B*ryce checked his watch more than a dozen times on Tuesday. She wasn't set to arrive for another couple hours, but the day was dragging, and he wished it was six already. He needed to get things out in the open and set things right. He had to tell her he'd made a mistake and apologize for taking advantage of her on New Year's. Yet at the same time, he was dreading this meeting. He was too old for her and still worried about her flirtatious behavior. He wanted to be sure he would never be burned again.

She was too opinionated, a strong-willed and capable woman, characteristics that served him well as an assistant, but he wasn't sure he wanted something like that in a romantic relationship.

The minutes passed slowly, but eventually the clock indicated it was time, and he was relieved when his secretary buzzed him. "Mr. Thomson? Ms. Winters has arrived."

"Send her in."

Carrie walked into his office with a pleasant look on her face, but nothing warm or welcoming, nothing to indicate she was excited to see him. That was good. It would be easier to apologize and make sure she understood where things stood. She was an employee and had to be reasonable enough to see that. He readjusted his own expression and turned into the businessman he needed to be.

He stood behind his desk so he wouldn't move over to her like he wanted to and take her hand in his. She placed the portfolio and plans on the desk and began going over the details.

Bryce sat down and waved her to sit as well, but she remained standing. He tried to dismiss it, but he could tell she wasn't comfortable with him, another thing that would help him in the conversation to follow. He would let her finish her update then tell her.

"Would you like me to contact Mrs. Alvey, or is that something you plan to do?" Carrie asked as she wrapped up her information.

Bryce looked at the name on the list, trying to remember who it was and what she wanted them to do. "I would appreciate you taking care of it." He couldn't concentrate on work with her in the room. She took every rational thought out of his mind and turned them on edge. He had to get back in control of the situation.

"Not a problem. I also have contacted the Taylors

and Mr. Byington. They are behind this one-hundred percent. You'll have this project off and running on schedule." Carrie took a slow step forward and leaned against the desk. "Is there anything else you need me to do?"

Bryce brought his steepled hands to his chin. "Actually, I need to speak with you. Please have a seat."

Carrie looked at the chair behind her where he'd pointed, the one that would give him the space he needed to say the next words, then sat down. "I wanted to apologize for what happened at the New Year's Eve party. It was an enjoyable evening, but I don't think we should go that route. I'm your employer. I should never have taken advantage of you like that. I promise it will never happen again."

She paused for a moment — smiling softly — then spoke hesitantly at first before hitting him in a rush with words he hadn't expected. "I had a wonderful time. I have never enjoyed dancing as much as I did that night. But I can't understand why you've been ignoring me. I thought we hit it off really well."

She smiled a tentative smile and though her hopeful expression played with his heart-strings, he had to stay strong. He couldn't let her do this to herself.

"You've been an excellent assistant, but I think the time is right for us to part ways on these projects."

"You're firing me?" Carrie's eyes widened a moment then they seemed to flash between disappointment and anger. Her gaze cleared, giving him a moment of panic, and she nodded.

"We both agreed this would be a trial run. You are a very capable assistant, but I think it's best if we stop working together."

"Why? Because we kissed? There's nothing wrong with that. I'm not going to sue you for sexual harassment, if that's what you're worried about."

Bryce blinked in surprise at the anger in her voice. "I didn't think you would. It's not about that." Bryce leaned forward, placing his hands on his desk while Carrie stared daggers at him. He cleared his throat. "It's just that you're so young. We would never work out that way. And I want to keep my relationship with Carlson on the best footing possible."

"You're firing me because I'm too young, and you want to kiss up to my boss?" Carrie's voice raised a little, and Bryce backpedaled.

"No, your age isn't in question. You're very capable, one of the best at what you do. I'm not your type, and I'm too old for you."

Carrie stood, placing her hands on the edge of his desk, and leaned toward him, her eyes full of fire. "Let me tell you something, *old man*. You're an idiot. If you think ten years is too much of an age difference, you might as well go pick out your casket, because you're obviously too old to live anymore."

She turned around and grabbed her purse. "And to think I wanted to date you because you happened to be a decent man, with morals, and goals in life. You help everyone around you, but are too stubborn to see that maybe someone could help you in life as well. If that's how you feel? Fine. I'll leave. I have another appointment I have to get to anyway. I'll text you the rest of the details and let you know what Mrs. Alvey says. I also have most of the plans taken care of for the exhibition, so you should be able to run things on your own if you don't keel over and die first."

"I didn't say I was—" Bryce began, but she cut him off.

"Goodbye, Mr. Thomson." Carrie turned on her heel and left his office, taking all the joy out of the room with her.

"Goodnight, Carrie," Bryce spoke as the door closed behind her.

He'd blown it big time. And before he could stand up to follow her out and beg her to forgive him and change his mind about everything, his secretary entered the room with a couple of folders and some details of phone calls he would have to address.

When he realized he would now have to take care of everything else on his own, he dropped his face into his hands and groaned. But it was for the best. It had to be.

***

Carrie wouldn't cry. She'd done enough of that already. Besides, the night dancing with Bryce wasn't that big of a deal. The fact that she had let it affect her so much was unbelievable. He obviously hadn't been bothered. But to fire her for being too young for him? It hadn't even been she who had initiated the kiss.

She forced that out of her mind. She wouldn't think about that anymore. She had to move on. Besides, it would be nice to not have to worry about making sure everything went according to plans. Yet, there were still a few things she had to take care of. He'd hired her to handle the publicity and make sure the event got the notice it deserved. She'd taken on a few extra things in the process. Most of those could be filled by Bryce's secretary. No, *Mr. Thomson's* secretary. She would stop thinking of the old fart by his name. If he wanted to be an old man, she'd think of him that way.

What kind of man in his mid-thirties thought he was too old? She shook her head and kept marching to her car. Carrie had an appointment with her nail salon and didn't want to be late. It was hard to get in to her favorite girl, and she wouldn't let a man get in the way of getting her nails done anymore. She was way overdue.

When she got into the salon and was seated in the chair with her hands on the little table, waiting for Angie, she shook her head. *Mr. Thomson will never get this project to go the way it should. I can't abandon the program yet.*

She would make sure this event still went off as she'd planned then leave Mr. Thomson to take care of the rest. But she would not let this go until it was done. She could handle working with him for a few more weeks. It wasn't like they saw each other in person anyway. It had all been done online or over the phone. When she was finished with her nails, she'd text him and tell him she was going to complete this before he could let her go. He owed her that much.

Besides, she wasn't doing this for him. Those kids were looking forward to showcasing their work, and she wanted to give it the best possible turnout.

"Hey, Carrie," Angie said. "How was your Christmas?"

"Great," Carrie said. "How about you?"

"It was nice." Angie took Carrie's hand in hers and pulled it closer to get a good look at her nails. "I went home to visit my parents and introduce them to Carlos."

"Ooh, that sounds serious." Carrie met Angie's eyes and knew from the smile covering Angie's face that things were going well with her relationship. "So tell me all about it."

Angie turned her hand a little, allowing Carrie to see the diamond on her finger. "He proposed on New Year's Eve."

Carrie grinned. "That's wonderful."

"It was the best night ever. So romantic. We went to the beach and walked for a while, then there was this cute little party set up with fires in barrels and some music. He says he didn't set it up, and that it just happened to be that way, but I think he did a little of the background. Then he got down on one knee and pulled out this gorgeous rock."

Carrie listened as Angie gave all the details, feeling happy for the girl, but she couldn't get the thoughts of Bryce out of her mind. When she'd told him about what a good time she'd had on New Year's, she'd seen a moment of agreement in his eyes. Then he'd told her she wasn't right for him. Maybe he was using his age as a gentle way to tell her they wouldn't work out. She was sure there was something else about her he didn't want. And that hurt. But she wouldn't change for a man. Her mother had tried that, tried giving up what was wonderful about her to get a man to love her, to stay with her when he obviously didn't want to.

Carrie would never go down that path. If Bryce didn't want her, she would survive. It would take a while to pull herself together, but she would not lose what made her who she was for a man. She took a shaky breath and blew it out slowly, hoping Angie wouldn't notice her lack of involvement in the conversation, then took another slow cleansing breath, thought of the ocean, and let the waves roll over her mind, washing away the irritation just like it had over the weekend.

When her nails were done, she pulled out her phone and sent a text before she changed her mind.

Carrie: Mr. Thomson, I will finish my commitment with this project.

As she arrived at her car, the buzz of a return text gave her a moment of hope, but when she read his simple message, she knew things were over.

Bryce: That is greatly appreciated.

Nothing more. She knew things were over, not that they had really been going anywhere, but now she knew there was no hope.

Chapter Twenty-Two

Carrie worked endless hours making sure everything was ready for the event. She got home late each night, partly to avoid any questions from Abby, who didn't understand why she didn't do something about Bryce. But she would not put herself out there for someone who didn't want her.

She would get over the disappointment of not being with him. Though she had come to enjoy the meetings and interactions she'd had with the man, she didn't need the stress. Besides, not every woman needed a man in her life. She was young enough; she still had time. According to Mr. Thomson, she was practically a baby.

It still burned when she thought about it, so she tried her best not to.

With the culminating event scheduled for tomorrow, she had one more day to make one last push of marketing. The kids and parents she was targeting seemed to interact well with the different hashtags and trending topics on the different social media sites.

Bryce had sent her one text to ask a question, but she'd called his secretary to give him the lengthy details, knowing she wouldn't have the patience to talk to him herself, even if he would take her call. Other than that, she had basically run this on her own, just like she would have if she'd still actually been employed by Mr. Thomson.

She wouldn't be getting paid for this, but it didn't matter. She loved the program so much, she was happy to donate these last days to it.

Carrie dragged herself into her apartment and wasn't surprised to see Abby on the couch watching her show and waiting for her to arrive. Instead of ignoring her roommate like she wanted to, Carrie dropped her bag, kicked off her heels, then joined Abby on the couch. She grabbed the second set of chopsticks and speared a piece of spicy chicken from the rare takeout boxes.

"A fat night tonight?" Carrie asked.

"Yeah, I caved," Abby said. "I've been craving this for a month. Figured I deserved it."

"Amen," Carrie said. "So, what's happening?"

Abby shifted a little, leaning against her to whisper some of the events on the show Carrie had missed over the last few weeks. When she'd been sufficiently informed, they watched until the commercial break, and Abby looked her over.

"So are you going to tell Bryce you'll give him another chance?"

Carrie rolled her eyes. "He doesn't want a chance. He's not interested."

"Yeah, that's a lie. He's just an idiot that doesn't know any better. I know he's into you. I could tell just from that one meeting at the gallery."

"Whatever. I'll see him once more tomorrow, then after that, it's over. I'm not going to go beg him to reconsider. It's not like we were anything anyway."

Abby shook her head. "If he thought about it enough to tell you that he's too old for you, it's likely he's thought it through to the point he's trying to convince himself he shouldn't."

"Exactly. He thinks he shouldn't. I'm fine with that. But if you would let it go, then maybe I can put it all behind me and move on to something else."

Abby snorted. "Like what?" She shoveled in some chow mein noodles then pointed the chopsticks at Carrie. "You never really dated anyway. Guys weren't your thing, but you never stopped talking about Bryce this and Bryce that. I know you were falling for him. I knew it before you'd been working with him for two weeks."

"I did not fall for him."

Abby raised an eyebrow then looked at the television, since the show had come on again. "You did. And I know you don't want to talk about it anymore. But if you don't do something about convincing him to give you two a chance, you're going to turn miserable. Just like he will. And you don't want that to happen."

Carrie sighed. "I'm beat. I'll see you tomorrow. You're still coming, aren't you?"

"Yeah. I'll be there."

Carrie considered her roommate for a moment. *Is she coming because she wants to make me talk to Bryce about our non-existent relationship?* Abby never glanced at her, instead kept her eyes glued to the show that Carrie had lost all interest in. She would never admit it, but she kind of wished she could convince Bryce to get over himself and see where things would lead.

He was everything she could want in a man, but she wouldn't embarrass herself by trying to win him over. Carrie worked her way into the kitchen and grabbed a yogurt out of the fridge. That would have to count for her dinner, along with what she'd stolen from Abby's meal.

On her way back through the front room, she paused a minute. "You seen Eric?"

Abby nodded, but didn't look away from the T.V. "He went out with a couple of friends. Said he'd be back late tonight."

"Thanks," Carrie said as she went into her room.

She'd ask him about how he was getting to the amateur artist debut tomorrow. For now, she just wanted to get a few hours of sleep. She had to be to Carlson's early to get all her stuff done in time to make it to the rec center and get the finishing touches on the event. She turned her phone to *Do Not Disturb* and crawled under her covers, hoping her mind would shut off long enough she could sleep.

***

Bryce woke to the sound of his cell phone ringing. He glanced at the clock and squinted to see the hour. A little past two a.m. If he'd had any living relatives, he would have been worried it was bad news. Not that anyone calling at two a.m. gave good news, but he wasn't overly concerned, more annoyed, and a little curious.

"Bryce," he said, hoping he didn't sound too groggy.

The connection wasn't the best, and a digitalized sounding voice asked if he would accept a collect call. The voice giving the name was slightly garbled, and Bryce said he'd accept the charges, even though he wasn't positive who it was.

"Mr. Thomson?" the familiar voice said, and Bryce tried to pinpoint where he knew it from.

"This is Bryce Thomson."

"I'm sorry to call you like this, but I've screwed up big-time, and I can't get ahold of Carrie."

Things clicked, and Bryce knew who it was. "Eric?" He sat up and adjusted the phone to his ear. "What's wrong?"

It took some coaxing and a couple of questions to get Eric to explain what had happened, but he finally learned Eric had been arrested for vandalism and hadn't been able to contact any family. Bryce wasn't sure what kind of things had happened in the boy's life, but he knew he didn't want any kind of interaction with his father, and, from what he'd gathered from Carrie, Eric's mom was dead. He lived with Carrie, who wasn't technically his guardian, but the closest he had to one.

"I'll be there as soon as I can. Don't talk to anyone without a lawyer."

"I know." Eric's voice sounded a little nervous, but not terrified, almost like he'd been through something like this before.

Bryce knew the kid had endured a tough childhood, but he hoped that by having his outreach program, they could make a difference in the lives of kids like Eric.

As he pulled on his pants and shoved his feet into his shoes, he wondered where Carrie was and why she hadn't answered her phone. Images of her on a date or out with some guy made his blood boil, and he wondered where that came from. He had no right to care where she was. But as he drove to the jail, he couldn't help wondering more about Carrie than he did Eric and his predicament.

Teen boys he could deal with. A grown woman he'd spurned scared him to death. If he helped Eric now, he would have to talk to Carrie too. There would be no ignoring her like he'd planned to do at the event later that night. *What am I getting myself into?*

Inside the jail was noisy, and a few people waited in line before he could get to the desk and tell them he was there to help Eric.

***

Bryce turned to Eric, glad he didn't have to stand outside the holding cell to talk. The officer knew Bryce was involved in the outreach program and had provided a room for them to talk in. "You sure you don't want me to go get her? I'm sure she'll understand."

Eric shook his head. "I don't want to overwhelm her today. She's got so much with this thing tonight."

Bryce tilted his head to the side and looked Eric over. "Maybe you should have thought of that before you got arrested. Don't you think she'll notice you aren't there?"

Eric hung his head.

"What went through your mind when you met up with those guys?" Bryce asked. He'd never gotten into trouble with the law — mostly because his dad would have killed him if he'd done something stupid like that. For another, he wasn't the daring kind of kid to try something reckless. Yet if he was going to be working with juveniles like this, he needed to know how to help them, to understand them.

"We just wanted to go have some fun."

Bryce studied Eric. "Being arrested and hanging out at the jail sounds like a blast. Is it?"

"Not really."

"So what are you going to do about this? You've got another entry in your record. I don't know much about your past, but from what I understand, you've had a little trouble before. That's why this time they'll probably press charges, and you've got a court date."

Eric groaned. "Carrie is gonna be ticked."

"She has a right to be. You were doing so well, and you're old enough to know better. To throw that all away for a little fun is a stupid and irresponsible thing to do." Bryce studied Eric, hoping his honesty wasn't going to drive the kid away. But he needed to be told straight out that if he didn't shape up, he'd be in some bigger trouble. "You're still a juvenile, so this won't carry on with you everywhere, but you have to make a choice now. Are you going to let your impulses get the best of you and possibly ruin your life, or are you going to man up and do something more useful with your life?"

Eric nodded thoughtfully but didn't answer.

"You take some time to think of what you're going to do about this."

"I will."

"Carrie's going to have to know. They won't release you to me since we aren't related." Bryce waited patiently for Eric's response. He finally lifted his head, looking confused and unsure of what to do.

"I don't know if they'll let me make another call since I used my call to get you after she didn't answer."

Bryce nodded. He figured they'd probably let him contact his sister, she was his relative after all, but he could probably get a hold of her sooner if he went to her house. "I'll go get her. She needs time to get this taken care of before too late in the day."

Eric nodded. "Thanks."

Bryce placed his hand on the kid's shoulder. "Learn from this. Don't let it break you, but don't waste this opportunity. Make a decision about how you're going to handle this, but know that it will affect you for the rest of your life." Bryce left the room, nodding to the officer outside the door. "I'll go find his sister so he can get processed and out of here. Thanks for the room."

The officer tilted his chin in acknowledgment then entered the room to get Eric and return him to his holding cell.

Bryce hoped the kid would make better choices from here on out. From what he gathered, Eric hadn't done any of the graffiti, but had been arrested on charges of vandalism and breaking city curfew. Maybe they could get a good lawyer to help sort things out. And, if Eric would do some community service hours, perhaps they'd reduce the fines and not actually put this mess on his records.

As he got in his car, the dark night looked to be working its way to the dawn. He hoped Carrie would be home. He called her number, but the phone went directly to voicemail. He took a slow breath. He would have to go to her house. He just hoped he wouldn't see her there with some guy.

Chapter Twenty-Three

*C*arrie's eyes flew open at the knock on her door. She turned over in her bed and looked at the clock on the nightstand. It wasn't even five a.m. *Who on earth is knocking at this hour?* She grabbed her robe and a decorative figurine with sharp points as she passed the front room on her way to the door. She peeked through the window and frowned at the sight of Bryce on her doorstep.

"What's going on?" Abby asked as she came into the room. She held a baseball bat and glared at the door. "Who is it?"

"Bryce," Carrie whispered.

"What's he doing here so early?" Abby asked, setting the tip of the baseball bat on the floor.

"I don't know." Carrie moved over to the door then glanced back at Abby. "Should I open it?"

Abby shrugged and leaned against the wall, resting her head as if she wished she were still asleep. At least she hadn't left the room and abandoned Carrie to Mr.

Thomson. Carrie hoped she wasn't just there to watch and see what Bryce would do —something she could misinterpret and tease Carrie about later.

Carrie opened the door, annoyance and frustration fighting for precedence, leaving little room for any other emotion. Yet embarrassment fought its way for control when she realized after she'd opened the door that she was only wearing her tank top and puppy-dog boxers under the robe that had managed to come untied.

"What do you want?" Carrie asked with a little more bite than necessary, but the embarrassment had fueled her anger.

Bryce blinked as he took her all in. She could see his eyes drawn to what the robe should have covered, but he quickly pulled his gaze back to her face, and she grabbed the edges of the robe and pulled it closed. Bryce swallowed then spoke. "I came to find you since Eric couldn't reach you."

"What?" Carrie turned around and looked at Abby. "Is Eric home?"

Abby turned around and moved over to Eric's door. She knocked as she opened it then turned around and shook her head. "His room's empty." Abby rushed back into the front room and approached the door.

Carrie turned back to Bryce. "What happened?"

"Can I come in?" Bryce asked. Carrie stepped back, and Bryce lifted his foot across the doorframe.

Abby placed her hand on Carrie's arm, and she appreciated the support.

"Is he hurt?" Carrie asked.

"No, he's fine. But he was caught with a couple of other kids doing some vandalism and is in jail."

"What?" Carrie said. "Why didn't he call me?"

"He tried, but your phone went to messages. Same with mine when I tried calling."

Carrie closed her eyes and let her head fall backward for a second before disentangling herself from Abby and moving into her room for her phone. She powered it on and turned back toward the front room as it came to life and produced the missing calls' log.

Carrie turned to Bryce. "I'm so sorry. I don't know what to say." She turned on the messages and listened to Eric tell her in a voice filled with shame and remorse that he'd done something stupid. She wished she would have answered the call instead of making him call Bryce. She didn't need his help, and she was sure Eric hadn't wanted to call his hero and tell him he'd screwed up. Now Bryce would think she wasn't a fit guardian for her brother. She looked at the man in front of her then realized that Eric had felt more comfortable calling him than his own brother. Bryce was a much better option than Shane any day.

"I went to the precinct to talk to him. They wouldn't release him to me, but I think we can convince them to lessen his charges, maybe even have him do community service hours. He wasn't actually the one to do the spray painting, but he was with them when they got caught. Kind of a wrong-place-at-the-wrong-time type thing, but he didn't stop them either, so he's not going to get off completely free of consequences."

Carrie nodded, not willing to speak.

"I can take you there if you'd like," Bryce offered.

Carrie blinked a few times as she processed her options. "Thanks, but I don't know how long I'll be, and I'll need to have my own car to get to the office afterward."

"I'll let you go then." Bryce turned to the door and glanced at her as if he wanted to say something, but then his gaze flitted to Abby before returning to Carrie. "If things don't clear up in time, don't worry about coming to the event tonight. I'm sure I can cover if you can't make it."

Carrie nodded numbly, feeling the complete dismissal from his life. When he closed the door behind him, she blinked back the tears and rushed to her room, feeling Abby follow her.

"How can I help?" Abby asked.

"Find me something to wear to the police station while I rush through the shower." Carrie wrapped her long hair in a bun so she wouldn't get it wet. She didn't have time to style it, but she didn't want to go out with sopping hair. By the time she finished her shower and quickly did her make-up, Abby had picked out a pair of slacks and nice blouse she could wear to the police station, then to the office afterward.

"Thanks, Abby. I'll call you if I need anything else."

"Good luck," Abby said as Carrie rushed out the door. Thoughts of Eric at the police station raced through her mind. She'd picked him up there once before and had sworn she would do everything she could to keep him away from there. Apparently, she'd failed. But the encouraging words from Bryce about the possibility of reducing his charges and getting him to do community service helped calm her nerves as she headed to the station.

***

Bryce watched her leave her house and get in her car. He had driven around the block, then parked where he could watch. He debated on following her to the police station, to try to help more, but he didn't think she wanted him there. When he'd told her about

Eric, she had looked mortified that he was aware of the situation, and he didn't want to make her worry he would be judging. He just hoped he could help.

He checked his schedule and knew if he wanted to give Carrie any help, the thing he would need to do was make sure the event went without a hitch tonight. He would do that for her so she could be free to take care of her family. He hoped she would still come tonight to see all her hard work.

***

As Carrie walked into the police station, she took a slow breath. She gave the front secretary her information, and they took her back to fill in the paperwork for getting Eric released. When everything was completed, an officer went to get Eric.

"I know I screwed up. I wasn't planning on doing it, but it kinda just happened."

Carrie blinked. "Just happened, huh." It sounded so much like what her father had said to her mother when he'd been caught cheating. "You just happened to break the law, spray painted someone's property."

"I wasn't the one doing it."

"But you were with them. You didn't stop it, and you broke curfew, even though you've been written up for that before."

Eric's gaze left hers, and he studied the floor.

"Is that really what you want to happen in your life? You want to give up control and let someone else dictate what happens next?"

Eric shrugged.

Carrie leaned forward, her voice low and bitter. "You want to give up control like Dad? End up in prison because you can't control yourself?"

Eric shook his head.

"'Cause if you don't watch yourself in little situations like this, you'll end up where you don't want to be." She took a slow deep breath, trying to calm herself. She was too young to be a parent, but Eric needed to have someone shake some sense into him. "I'm not your mom. I've tried to be a good big sister and help you out, but if you keep doing this, there won't be anything I can do to save you. The judge is not going to look on this lightly. Eric, you've already had a warning. This time it's too far, and you know it."

"I know. I'm sorry."

Carrie sighed. "I hope so."

Eric's shoulders sagged. His face looked so sad and embarrassed that Carrie couldn't help but feel sorry for him. She moved over to him, put her arm around him, and gave him a gentle squeeze but didn't say anything.

He shook his head. "I know I should have told them no. I should have left when I saw what they were up to, but they were my ride, and I didn't want to walk home or call you to come get me."

She gritted her teeth, just waiting for him to complain about not having a car, but instead he took a slow shaky breath. "I'm sorry, Carrie."

She nodded. "I know. Let's go home."

Eric followed her out to the car and slid into his side without a word. He'd tell her more about it when he was ready, and right now, she didn't know if she wanted to hear any excuses anyway. She glanced at him and could tell from the drooping eyelids that he wouldn't be able to really tell her much without getting some rest.

"I'll drop you off at home, then I need to go into the office to get a few things caught up. I'll be back around five or so. I want you to be ready to head to the rec center so you can help with the setup of your display."

"We did that last night."

Carrie glanced at him then turned her attention back to the road. "Not all of the artwork has been set up completely. I was going to go make sure it got finished before the event begins. So you can help with that."

Eric ducked his head, not looking at her.

"We're going," Carrie said gently, but with enough steel in her voice he would know she was serious. "This is my last event with the program. I intend to be there, and so will you. You've got to be there to answer questions about your project anyway."

"No one's going to care if I don't show up."

Carrie looked at him and caught his eye for a moment before he looked away again. "I care, and so will Mr. Thomson. We're going."

Eric nodded, and she focused on the road trying to ignore his giant yawn reminding her of how little sleep she'd had and how long it would be before she could go to bed tonight. Yet, she could make it through the rest of the day. After tonight, she would be much freer. She'd catch up on her sleep then.

Chapter Twenty-Four

*C*arrie couldn't wait for the day to be over. She'd finally gotten all the client accounts updated and finished her to-do list that had been plaguing her for days. After tonight, she wouldn't have to speak with Bryce Thomson again, and she could have a social life once more.

She rushed home and showered quickly then pulled her hair in an intricate twist and slipped into her dress for the evening. She didn't have to look as fancy as other events, but she still needed to look like a hostess of a gallery event, not just an employee at work.

She knocked on Eric's door, and when he didn't answer, she peeked into his room. It didn't look like he'd been there for a while. She pulled out her phone and texted him.

Carrie: Where are you? We need to leave right now.

His response took a while, so she muttered under her breath about him while she grabbed something quick to eat, glad Abby hadn't eaten all the takeout from last night. She would have to order in next time to pay her back.

By the time his answer came through, Carrie had finished eating and brushed her teeth, ready to kill the kid.

Eric: Already here.

Carrie wondered how he'd made it there, since he didn't have a car, or why he'd gone on his own when he hadn't wanted to go earlier. Maybe he'd gotten a ride with a friend from the program.

Carrie: Why didn't you tell me you were going early?

Eric: Sorry, they said they needed a little help to finish the displays. So I came.

Carrie sighed in frustration. She didn't know what to do with her brother at the moment. She put that out of her mind and grabbed her bag and a fresh can of soda then headed out to the car. She took a long drink of the Dr. Pepper, hoping to numb some of the butterflies creeping into her stomach. It helped a little, but the closer she got to the rec center and the man she'd been trying to avoid in person and in thought, the more they took flight.

She swallowed hard and gave herself a pep talk. *I can do this. He'll want to avoid me just as much as I do him.* Probably more, in fact, given the way he had hardly responded to any of the communications on this event. She forced him out of her thoughts once again. This was about kids like Eric, ones who needed something good in their lives to stay out of trouble. Something to feel proud of.

As she drove to the rec center, she thought of all the kids who had been there over the last few months. It had been amazing to see them get into their creativity. She was sad she wouldn't be able to interact with them as closely now that she would no longer be working for Mr. Thomson, but she could still come on occasion. She'd had a lot of fun doing the classes on graphic design. She could still volunteer to teach some classes. Bryce wouldn't be there all the time.

Carrie breathed a little easier and worked her way through traffic, finding herself turning into the parking lot before she knew she was there.

She climbed out of the car, adjusted her dress and grabbed her purse, then dropped her keys into it after locking the car. She could see a few of the youth gathered already. One or two were carrying some artwork. She hurried forward to reach the building before they got there. As she held the door open for the kids, she saw Eric sitting on the front bench. She smiled at him, and he smiled back, halfheartedly. He was trying, and that made her anger and annoyance at him dissipate.

She wanted to grab him and pull him into another hug, but she knew he didn't want anything like that. He didn't want her to be his mom, but she didn't want to let him think he didn't have anyone to help him.

It was hard to be his guardian, especially when he first came to live with her after he'd gotten in trouble while living with their dad. Carrie was glad her father had lost his parental rights, though having them taken away because he was in prison hadn't been all that nice. Eric had suffered by getting involved in the lifestyle their dad had introduced him to, but he had been doing so well. Maybe this remorse was a good thing. Maybe he really was changing.

Carrie joined him on the bench and studied him for a minute. She knew it was the best she could ask for. At least he wasn't refusing completely... and at least he was here at the event instead of running the streets.

"Is your artwork hung?" she asked.

He nodded.

"Good. Do you know what else needs to be done?"

"Not much, Mr. T. and some of the other kids took care of most of it."

He followed her into the little office she had used with Mr. Thomson where she tucked her purse into the filing cabinet he'd set aside for her use. She would need to remember to empty out the few things she had brought and left there. But maybe not tonight. If this event went like she hoped it would, there would be so much going on that it would be as much as she could do to keep up with it all.

Hopefully, this would show the City Arts Alliance that Mr. Thomson's idea of creating a community theater where they could get the kids from the area involved would be in the best interest of the city.

She was sure they were almost ready to take it to the city offices for a vote. Tonight would be the final push. She put her game face on and walked back out into the hallway. She glanced behind her to make sure Eric was following and turned her head back around in time to see a rock-solid chest in front of her.

She slammed into the familiar suit and felt Bryce's arms as they wrapped themselves around her to steady the two of them so she didn't knock him down.

She took a few quick steps, trying to get her balance, and hoped she didn't step on his feet in the process. His hands slowly pulled away from her upper arms where they had come to rest.

"Ms. Winters," he said, "I'm glad you could make it."

Carrie only nodded, not sure she could get a word out around the embarrassment enveloping her. She stepped back and was saddened by the emptiness she felt when his hands fell completely away. He shouldn't affect her like that, but the only thing she could remember was when they had danced so closely at the New Year's Eve party. She chanced a glance at him and saw that his face looked unaffected. The butterflies that had once taken flight were now dead in the pit of her stomach. He truly was completely over her. In fact, he didn't look at her longer than a few seconds before turning his attention to Eric.

"How are you?" Bryce asked.

"Good. Thanks again for your help last night."

"No worries." Bryce nodded. "That's what I'm here for."

Eric shuffled his feet. "We were just going to make sure the displays were all up." He took a step down the hallway toward the main room where the artwork was displayed.

Carrie watched as Bryce studied Eric's back, then he glanced at her for a moment. "I'll let you get to it then." He took a step away, and Carrie frowned then followed Eric, putting more distance between her and Bryce.

Why did I have to slam against him? It only proved to her what she'd been trying to deny for so long. She wanted him to want her. She didn't care what he said about their age differences, but it was obvious he had no feelings for her. And to add to the list of reasons he wouldn't want her, it had been her own brother who had needed help and couldn't stay out of trouble. She could hardly face him. It was a good thing this was her last night. And if it weren't for the fact that the mayor and the arts alliance was going to be here tonight, she would have left him to do this alone, since apparently, that was the way he preferred to be.

But she would stay for her brother and the other youth. Besides, she did owe him for helping Eric last night.

***

Bryce's hands tingled as he remembered the softness of her skin. It had been torture to hold Carrie, and even more so to let her go. He had been a fool to think he didn't need her. She was young, sure, but she definitely showed more maturity than most women her age. She was working two jobs, taking care of her younger brother, and still volunteering for this event, even though he'd told her they shouldn't work together anymore.

He clenched his hands into a fist then tried to shake out the feeling of her. Yet his hands itched to touch Carrie again. He turned around to watch her as she worked with each of the youth who had already arrived. He was sure she was coaching them on how to interact with the people who would be coming to see their work. The woman was a natural, and the kids all seemed to relax after they had talked to her.

Eric was obviously embarrassed about what had happened, but Carrie and Eric seemed to have come to some kind of understanding about the whole thing. The kid seemed contrite enough, and he hoped the conversation they had had would help him make better choices. He should have known better, especially since he'd had some trouble of a similar sort before he came to live with Carrie.

Bryce wanted to do more, but knew that getting involved wouldn't help. It would probably make Carrie angry at him. *No, from here on out, Carrie will have to be in control.* She would be the one to go with him to his court date. Bryce would let the kid's lawyer know that he would accept community service for the program if the judge would agree.

With Carrie here tonight, he had little that he needed to do on his own since the youth had all finalized the displays after he'd rallied them earlier. Yet as he watched her take over, he once again regretted insisting they shouldn't work together. As these types of projects kept going, he would be much busier, and he doubted he'd do as good of a job as she had. The only reason he'd been able to get the kids going on this tonight was because of all her groundwork.

It was for the best to end their relationship. Touching her for just those few moments was too much of a reminder of what things could turn into if he kept working with her. He would eventually cave and ask her out if he didn't make sure she wasn't anywhere near him. *Out of sight, out of mind.*

But, as she walked past his view on her way to another group of youth, he knew he was lying to himself. He would never forget her. And if he wasn't a coward, he would go tell her that. But the way she had stepped away from him as if burned when they'd run into each other outside the office, he knew she didn't feel the same way. He'd blown his chance, and tonight would not be the time to try again, not when she had so much on her plate.

Chapter Twenty-Five

The night flew by, and before Carrie knew it, the kids were leaving with parents, and the director of the arts alliance was shaking her hand while the mayor was leading Bryce toward where she stood. She had done her best to avoid being too close to Bryce all night, though she couldn't help watching him. He seemed to be a lot more at ease than the first time she'd come to one of his events.

She had caught him watching her a couple of times, but he always looked away before making eye contact. She tried not to let it bother her, but through the first half of the event, she wished she could go talk to him, corner him in his office and thank him for helping Eric while she was unavailable… to tell him that she wanted to stay a part of this outreach program, even if he didn't want to employ her. She'd volunteer because she wanted kids like Eric to have a better place to be than running the streets, to make sure they had a creative outlet for all the energy and creativity bursting inside of them. But as the night progressed, he'd kept his distance, and she knew it wouldn't be a good idea. She'd only succeed in embarrassing herself.

Now that this event was done, nothing would force them together. Still, she watched him closely as he and Mayor Larsen approached her. He met her eyes for a moment then looked at the mayor who was still speaking. Bryce nodded, and Carrie turned her attention back to Mrs. Alvey.

"Ah, here's the mayor."

Carrie waited for them to arrive, and she smiled and took the man's outstretched hand. "Good to see you again tonight, Mayor Larsen."

"This project was amazing. To actually talk to the kids who created these pieces was interesting. I think you've got something wonderful going on here, and I hope to see it continue to grow." He turned to Mrs. Alvey. "What do you think? Is the funding there to help support this?"

Mrs. Alvey nodded. "I think we can work things out to cover a portion of this. We'll still need to count on some donations and support from local businesses, but with how much you've done on this outreach program and the overwhelming support and backing by the parents, schools, and neighboring businesses here, I think it would be foolish of us to not do more to help." She took a step closer to Bryce. "Your idea for a community theater and musical program is something I'd like to see more of. If you could get us a proposal with the details of materials needed, we'll discuss it at our next board meeting and give you an answer."

Bryce shook her hand and glanced at Carrie. She wasn't sure what he was thinking as he looked at her, maybe wondering if he could get her to write up the proposal, but she would stay far away from that. The more she did to help him, the harder it would be to stay away.

Carrie caught sight of Eric, who was watching her and the group around her from the wall where his artwork hung. She exchanged a few more pleasantries with the mayor before excusing herself while Bryce was busy with the arts alliance director.

She moved across the floor and joined Eric. "You ready to go home?"

Eric looked around the room. "Don't you have to help out more?"

Carrie shook her head. "I no longer work for Mr. Thomson. This was the last event, and he is capable of taking care of the rest now that all the guests are gone."

Eric nodded thoughtfully but didn't move from the wall.

"Did you want to stay?" Carrie asked.

Eric nodded. "I kinda feel like I should help with the cleanup."

Carrie studied her brother for a moment. She had never known him to volunteer for extra work, not that he was lazy or anything, but unless it was required, he never offered. Maybe he was growing up or just getting ready to do his community service hours. She nodded. "I guess that would be a good idea."

"Thanks," he whispered.

Carrie took stock of the room. There were very few people still there, many were the staff Mr. Thomson had hired to clean up and the caterers he'd brought in for the light refreshments. They would take care of the food detail and the sweeping, but Carrie and Eric could do something with the chairs and tables.

She kicked off her heels and put them against the wall. She loved shoes but really enjoyed the feel of being free of them after a long night.

Carrie and Eric worked quietly, organizing the tables and chairs and moving the displays back into the classrooms where they could be locked up. Before they were halfway done, she noticed Bryce had joined them and was working close to Eric. They talked in hushed voices, and Eric glanced at Carrie a few times. She hoped they weren't talking about her then shook her head. Eric would probably be thanking Bryce for his help without talking too loud to be overheard by anyone.

She studied them for a moment. Eric's shoulders sagged, and Bryce clapped him on the back in an encouraging way. Her heart softened again, and she wished she hadn't seen that. It was easy to tell herself she never wanted to see the jerk again, but when he played the good guy, she wished she could have a different outcome to their relationship.

They stayed for about thirty minutes before nothing was left for them to do. Eric approached Mr. Thomson, and Carrie stayed back, letting them have time to talk again. She took the chance to go to the office she'd kept her stuff in and gathered most of it. A small box helped keep it all together, and she left the office for the last time.

Eric met her in the hallway near the front lobby area and opened the door for her as she approached then took the box out of her hands once she'd stepped outside and led the way to the car.

"Thanks for the help tonight," Carrie said. She opened the back door for him to put the box inside.

"It was fun," Eric said as he stood back up straight with empty hands.

Carrie smiled. "You did a good job. I saw you talking to a lot of visitors. They seemed impressed with your art."

Eric smiled. "Yeah, and it made me decide something."

Carrie waited, leaning her hip against the front door of the car.

Eric looked at the rec center then back at her. "I've decided I don't want anyone else to make decisions for me. I want to be in control, and I won't do anything stupid like last night, ever again."

"I'm glad," Carrie said.

"Thanks for not giving up on me," Eric said. "It means a lot that you and Mr. T. didn't freak out about it."

"I did freak out," Carrie said. "I was so ticked at you."

"I know, but you didn't kick me out like Shane did." Eric looked at his shoes again.

Carrie took a step closer and hugged him in the middle of the parking lot, not caring who would see. She needed it, even if he didn't. "I don't ever want to be compared to Shane," Carrie said.

"I don't ever want to be compared to Dad again. I'll do everything I can to be different than him." Eric said, pulling back from the hug.

Carrie let him go and bit her lip. "Sorry about that."

"You were right. And I needed to hear it."

"Let's go home. I think I need a huge bowl of ice cream."

Eric grimaced.

"Don't tell me. You ate it all, didn't you?" Carrie cocked her head to the side, staring at him.

"Sorry."

"You'll just have to run into the store and get me some."

"Deal," Eric said. "What flavor?"

Carrie thought for a moment. "Double-double chocolate fudge."

Eric frowned, and Carrie chuckled.

"You don't have to eat it. Besides, it's my treat for surviving the day."

She turned back to look at the rec center with a strange mix of emotions running through her, sadness that she wouldn't be as involved in the program, though she hoped she could still volunteer on occasion, but stronger was the feeling of satisfaction. She had taken this project further than what Bryce could have done on his own, and the changes in the lives of kids like Eric would be immeasurable.

She pulled out her phone and sent what she figured would be her last text to Bryce.

Carrie: It was a pleasure working with you. Thank you for the experience. Good luck in your future endeavors.

***

Bryce stood near the window looking out into the parking lot, watching Carrie and Eric as they stood by her car. He wished he had a valid reason to actually go to her. He had almost convinced himself to approach her at least a dozen times throughout the night. Then when she'd left the conversation with the mayor and the arts alliance director, he'd wished he could have left them right then. But he'd needed to secure their support. Now, Eric needed the time to come clean and make things right with his sister.

Bryce turned away from the window to start locking up. His phone buzzed just as he lifted a box to take out to his car. He exited the back door to the employee parking area and slid the box into the back seat then pulled out his phone.

The text from Carrie caught him off guard, and he stared at it for a moment. *I can't let her go.* She was the best thing that had ever happened to the outreach program, and if he was honest, to him as well.

He made a snap decision to follow her home.

He tried to convince himself it was because he wanted to thank her for her hard work — for going above and beyond the job requirements — and make sure she was compensated for her efforts, but he would add a bonus to the last paycheck and deposit into her account anyway. He didn't need to do this in person.

But throughout the twenty minute drive, he never once could make himself stop following her and turn around, not even when she'd pulled into the grocery store and run in with Eric. Within minutes, she returned and headed toward her home again. It was as if his car had a mind of its own or was attracted to hers like a magnet. He tried not to follow too closely behind, but he didn't want to lose her in the dark.

As Carrie pulled into her driveway, he stopped his car a few houses down from hers then shut off his lights and watched as Eric got out of the car and headed to the house. He waited to see Carrie get out, but her door never opened, and he watched as her head bowed over her steering wheel.

Is she okay?

He watched for more than five minutes, not sure what she was doing. Her head bent on occasion, but mostly she leaned it back against the headrest. He looked toward her house, and Eric didn't seem to notice she hadn't come in. *Did he go to bed without even caring that his sister is still out here?*

The weather was cool, but not too cold, yet her car wasn't running as far as he could tell. Carrie was still in her sleeveless dress, and he worried about her. Bryce got out of his car and slowly walked toward her house. He didn't want to scare her, but he had to find out if she was okay. The sound of epic love ballads vibrated from her car.

He watched her head to see if she moved it at all. In the side mirror, he could see her face. Her eyes were closed as her head rested against the back of her seat, and she looked unhappy. He had never seen her frown before, not even when he'd told her they couldn't see each other.

No, that face had been full of fire and disbelief, but she had never looked sad. Now, Carrie just looked so fragile he wanted to pick her up and hold her. On the passenger seat sat an empty pint-size container of ice cream. Maybe she had stayed in the car to eat the ice cream and listen to music.

Before he could stop himself, he knocked on her window.

Carrie startled inside and threw one hand over her heart, then she scrambled to lock the car door before she finally registered who he was. When her eyes lit with recognition, she scowled then shook her head. She rubbed her hands across her face then opened the door and got out.

Bryce stepped back to give her room, but didn't retreat from the annoyance in her eyes.

"What the heck do you think you're doing? You scared me to death. Why are you here?"

"I…" Bryce fumbled for something to say. "…I wanted to thank you."

"By making me think I was being attacked in my own driveway?" She scowled at him.

"I wasn't attacking you."

Carrie shook her head. "Why are you here?"

Bryce looked toward her house then back at her. "I wanted to make sure you two were okay."

Carrie looked at the house too, probably thinking about Eric. "We're fine." She took a slow breath then let it out with a heavy sigh. "Thank you for helping him. I'm sorry I didn't have my phone on, and he had to call you."

"I didn't mind. I'm glad he felt comfortable calling me. I wanted to be a support for kids in the program."

Carrie nodded. "Well, you apparently did a good enough job with Eric." She cocked her head to the side. "Have you had any other kids call you for help?"

Bryce shook his head. "Not yet."

Carrie crossed her arms over her chest and rubbed her bare arms. Bryce took his suit coat off and took a step closer to her. When she didn't argue, he wrapped the jacket around her bare shoulders and could see her practically melt into the warmth still clinging to it from his body.

"If you keep up like this, I'm sure you'll be having more coming to you for help." She looked at him. "You sure you're ready for that?"

Bryce shrugged. "I didn't start this program to keep things easy in my life."

Carrie raised her brows. "You wanted things to get stressful?"

Bryce took a small step forward to meet her gaze better. "I wanted to be useful, to be a part of something bigger."

"Oh."

"I'm used to being alone."

Carrie's eyes hardened. "Apparently."

"But what I'm not used to is feeling lonely." He took another tiny step forward, not daring to go too fast but wishing to get closer to her. She wasn't leaning against her car, but she was close to it, and if he pushed too fast, she might leave.

"So why did you push me away?" Carrie asked. She was standing her ground, and that gave him hope. She wasn't going to run from him, but she wasn't going to let him get out of answering.

"I don't know. I told myself all kinds of reasons. But honestly, the truth is I was a fool."

Carrie's lip twitched into an almost smile. At least she wasn't frowning anymore. "Well, old people aren't supposed to be foolish. So what excuse do you have for that?"

Bryce smiled then took a small step forward, close enough to be almost touching her. She still didn't step back but held herself firmly in place, and he found it incredibly attractive. "Maybe I'm not really all that old."

Carrie smiled and studied his face. She reached out her hand, tentatively took his chin in her palm, and turned his face to the side. Then, after a moment, turned it the other way so she could look at his other cheek. "I don't see any gray in your hair, but the light out here isn't the best, so I can't be sure." She ran her finger across his cheek and tapped his temple by his eyes softly. "No wrinkles either."

"Thank heavens." Bryce took her hand in his then trapped it against his face. Her fingers were cool, but his face felt hot under her touch. He leaned closer until his forehead almost touched hers. "Do you think you can forgive me for my temporary lapse in judgment?"

Carrie pulled back a little, but only enough to look him in the eyes. "Depends."

"On what?" He still had her hand in his but had pulled it away from his face and held it in front of him near his heart.

"On what you actually mean by this lapse in judgment. What do you want from me?" Carrie studied him, and he prepared himself to beg.

"I want to take you out — on a date, not a business dinner either. I want to talk to you about your life, your hopes and dreams. Tell you some of mine. Find out if we are compatible in more than just a business arrangement."

"So you aren't trying to hire me again because you realize how much you can't do without me?" Her eyes sparkled with amusement, but he could still see the hint of fear behind them.

Bryce shook his head. "I can't do without you — but not just at work. I miss you… the happy personality you have… the joy you bring into the room the moment you step into it. I miss the strength you have as you work with the troubled kids, and even your ability to take care of your brother on your own."

Carrie glanced behind her toward the house, and Bryce took her chin in his hands to turn her back to him. "He told me all about how you took him in. He was so devastated to think he'd let you down. We had a good discussion. I think he'll be fine."

Carrie sighed and rested her head against his palm.

He brought his other hand to her face and cupped her cheeks between his hands. "You are an incredible woman, and I'm ashamed to admit I almost let you go without a fight. I want to make that right. I want a chance to date you, to prove you can trust me, to see where we can go together."

Carrie closed her eyes, and Bryce wished he knew if it was an invitation to kiss her, or if she was trying to find a way to let him down.

"Tell me I have a chance," Bryce pleaded.

Carrie opened her eyes, and Bryce's heart thudded when he saw the mirth behind them. "I think we'll need to do a test."

"What kind of test?"

"Well, it's three parts." She placed her hands against his chest and gripped him by the shirt, pulling him toward her for a kiss.

Just before his lips touched hers, he prayed with all his might that he would pass this test. The moment his mouth claimed hers — or hers claimed his; he wasn't sure exactly who was in control here — he just let things go as they would.

She eventually pulled away and rested her head against his chest, her breaths coming at the same gulping pace as his own.

"I wasn't worried about you passing that part," Carrie said after a moment, and Bryce chuckled as Carrie giggled while she gripped him around the chest, holding on to him as if she might fall over if she let go. He was glad she was steadying him, because he had never felt this way after a kiss. Though, that was no ordinary kiss. Even the fantastic kisses on New Year's didn't hold a candle to this.

After a moment, he whispered into her hair. "What's the next part of the test?"

Carrie giggled again. "Well, you've got to watch another movie with me."

Bryce sighed. "Is it like the one from Thanksgiving?"

Carrie snorted, and Bryce thought it was adorable. She shook her head. "No, the movie itself isn't the test."

"What is then?"

"We've got to see if you're young enough to stay awake through it. You know it's pretty late."

Bryce shook his head. "Are you ever going to let me live that down?"

Carrie paused as if considering it. "No, probably not. And that's the other test. Can you handle me? I'm not going to change who I am."

Bryce placed his hands on her shoulders and looked her straight in the eye. "I would never want you to change. I fell in love with you, not some particular version of you. Everything about you — from the big sister, to the employee, to the friendly girl, to the fabulous hostess, to the collected woman even after an injury, to the passionate kissing… and the crazy movies with made-up dialogue."

"You fell in love with me?" Carrie asked, her eyes bright as if filling with tears.

"I did."

"When?" She studied him. "Because I wasn't sure I loved you until after you'd fired me for wanting to protect me from some lecherous old man."

Bryce shook his head, chuckling at the adorable pest in his arms. He would do everything he could to prove he wasn't too old for her. To start, he would kiss her senseless again.

When he finally pulled back, he took her hand in his, mostly as a way to keep himself from pulling her against him again. "We'd better get started on that movie, so I have a chance to pass this test of yours."

Carrie walked with him to the house and opened her door, but, before she stepped inside, she looked at him. "My roommate is here, my brother is here, and I'm inviting you in to watch a movie, but we can't let it go farther. Are you okay with that?"

Bryce nodded. "We have all the time in the world, because, even though I've got just a touch of a head start, I'm hoping to grow old with you."

Epilogue

Carrie fingered the necklace Bryce had given her for Valentine's Day almost two months ago. She had told him she didn't need any fancy jewelry, but she realized she had lied when she opened the velvet box at the restaurant. It was gorgeous, and not one of the common diamonds pushed at all the jewelry stores and through every possible media outlet. She was so sick of looking at the benign necklaces promising "*happiness ever after.*" This one had small stones of different colors in a beautiful rainbow pattern, making her think of the painting he'd given her for Christmas.

Though he was rich enough to buy her whatever she wanted, he never used his money to try to convince her to stay with him. Instead, he'd showed her each day how precious she was to him. He took her for walks, went bike riding with her on the trails outside the city, took her to museums, and listened to her as she told him what she thought of the pieces. He'd even come this weekend to the beach and tried surfing.

She sat on the bench outside her hotel room as Bryce showered in his room next door. Eric had accompanied them and was sharing Bryce's room so Kourtney could share Carrie's. They were still going strong, and Carrie knew Kourtney was a good influence for him. She hoped Eric would keep improving at his schoolwork. He'd done his community service and had paid his debt to society, and, with Bryce vouching for him, the judge had been lenient.

They owed Bryce a lot. Carrie watched the waves roll in and chuckled at the memory of him trying to surf for the first time. Eric had thought it was hilarious the first few times he'd wiped out, but a couple of hours into it, Bryce had managed to catch a few waves large enough to impress her brother… and her.

Carrie's thoughts were interrupted when Bryce opened his motel room door. She smiled up at him, and he slid onto the bench next to her. She rested her head on his shoulder, and he winced. Though he'd acted tough around Eric, his muscles were, no doubt, screaming in pain from all the roughness they'd suffered.

"Sorry." Carrie tugged on his arm. "Here, come sit in front of me, I'll give you a massage."

"You don't have to do that."

"I know, but I want to. I can't help myself when there's a hunk of a man right by me."

259

"I'll bet you say that to all the guys."

Carrie placed her hands on his shoulders, leaned forward, and kissed him softly on the neck. "Nope, just to you."

"Thank you."

Carrie pressed her fingers deep into his muscles, massaging the shoulders and neck, then moving down to his upper biceps. She leaned against his back as she reached for his forearms and worked her way back up slowly to the shoulders and neck again, then down his broad back.

He sighed in pleasure, sending shivers down Carrie's spine. It took all she had to keep the massage contained to just his back and shoulders when all she wanted to do was wrap herself around him and disappear into his embrace. It was getting harder and harder to keep her hands off him, and she knew he was trying just as diligently to keep things in check each time they saw each other.

She eased up on the massage and lightly scratched his back. He leaned his head against her leg, and she played with his hair, still damp from his shower.

The sun was still high enough they had a few more hours before sunset, but Carrie would be content enough to sit here like this until the sun had submerged itself into the ocean in front of them.

Instead, Bryce stood up and took her hand in his.

"Care to take a walk with me?"

Carrie slipped her flip-flops on and turned to the door to tell Eric where they were going.

Bryce kept hold of her hand. "I've already told him we'd probably go for a walk to the beach. He was going to order pizza later for dinner. Did you want to join them or go somewhere else?"

"Pizza's good."

"Great, we can walk for as long as we want then."

She fell into step with him, and they crossed the parking lot, then the road, and worked their way down the path until they reached the sand. She took off her flip-flops, and he did the same. She led him to the water's edge where the sand was firmer, and they walked for miles before eventually turning around to make their way back. They didn't speak much, just walked in comfortable silence, broken occasionally by an observation of the scenery. She hadn't expected this day to be so perfect, but the weather had been nice, the crowds small, the company enjoyable. She didn't think anything else could make this day any better.

Bryce squeezed her hand, and she squeezed back. "Are you cold?" Bryce asked.

"No, it feels good." Carrie looked at the sun as it lowered itself in the sky. It wouldn't be long before it was resting on the water. They would need to head inside soon, but they were less than a mile from their motel. "We should probably get back though. If Eric ordered the pizza already, it might be gone by now."

"Don't worry. I'll order you a new one."

"My hero," Carrie said, grabbing his arm and hugging it a moment as she rested her head against him. "What would I do without you?"

"You'd manage," Bryce said. He paused a moment then stopped her and turned her to face him. "I don't know if I could manage without you, though."

"You did for all those years before. I'm sure you'd figure it out."

"What if I don't want to?" Bryce asked. "What if I don't want to let you go ever again? What if I don't want to room with your brother the next time we come to the beach? What if I wanted to bring my wife with me?"

Carrie's eyes widened and Bryce hurried to clarify. "I'm talking about you. I'm no longer married, you know that, right?"

Carrie nodded, unable to keep the smirk off her face. "Yeah, I'm aware of that."

Bryce sighed in frustration. "I'm not doing a very good job of this. What I'm trying to say is… will you marry me?"

Carrie smiled. "Oh, that's what you were trying to say." Though her words came out calm and clear, her heart was in her throat. *He wants to marry me.* She would be his forever, and the thought of that brought her more joy than she'd expected.

Bryce watched her with a touch of fear or maybe trepidation in his eyes. She wanted to hug him for how adorable he looked. He had no idea how perfect he was for her. She tucked herself against his chest, wrapping her arms around his back, feeling his heart beat against her cheek.

"I love you, Bryce, even more than I thought I could. I'll marry you on one condition."

"What's that? Should we go find a movie to rent?" He tried to sound lighthearted, but Carrie could feel his nervousness.

Carrie chuckled then looked up at him. "Tempting, but no. My condition is that it's forever. I know you were hurt, and I've seen how much it hurt my mom when my dad left her. If we have kids, they need both of us – always. If I marry you, we're in it for the long haul. I'm sure we'll have issues, but I think we can make it if we are both fully committed to it. Are you in all the way?"

Bryce nodded. "Absolutely. I'll never let you go and will fight for you every day."

Carrie smiled. "I'll make sure what we have together is worth fighting for."

"Darling, you already have."

Dear Reader,

I hope you enjoyed reading *Winter's Kiss*. Please consider posting a review or rating on Amazon or Goodreads. Reviews help spread the word. It's the best way to say "thank you" to any author.

If you have questions or comments, please feel free to contact me at authorlaurabastian@gmail.com

Find me on:
www.lauradbastian.com
www.facebook.com/AuthorLauraBastian

Thanks for reading.

Acknowledgments

So many people go into the creation of a book, from the person who sparks the idea, to the friends who let me pester them asking for help, advice, tips, and so much more. Cindy, Jaclyn, and Lindzee are some of my favorite go-to helpers in books like this. I couldn't do without the brainstorming, beta reads, and advice on writing romance as well as more formatting tips. And to my chat room buddies in the Sprintwriters Central website for the cheer leading.

Mom, you know I love you. Thanks for all the praise that still makes me grin like a little girl.

And as always, thanks to my husband and children who tolerate my absence when I'm totally immersed in writing and revisions and who only roll their eyes just a little when I tell them, no this story doesn't have any magic in it either. Just more kissing.

About Laura D. Bastian

Laura grew up in a small town in central Utah and now lives in another small town in northern Utah. She always loved stargazing and imagining life out-side her own little world. A graduate of Utah State University with a degree in Elementary and Special Education, Laura has been using that training as she raises her children and writes make believe worlds. You can usually find her on her laptop either typing away, or on social media interacting with friends when she's not playing in her garden.